"The Country of the Blind"
and Other
Science-Fiction Stories

H. G. WELLS

Edited by

MARTIN GARDNER

DOVER PUBLICATIONS, INC.
Mineola, New York

DOVER THRIFT EDITIONS

GENERAL EDITOR: PAUL NEGRI

Bibliographical Note

This Dover edition, first published in 1997, is a new selection by Martin Gardner of six stories reprinted from standard sources. Mr. Gardner has also written a new general introduction and introductions to each story specially for this edition.

Library of Congress Cataloging-in-Publication Data

Wells, H. G. (Herbert George), 1866–1946.
   "The country of the blind" and Other Science Fiction Stories /
H. G. Wells ; edited by Martin Gardner.
      p.   cm. — (Dover thrift editions)
   ISBN 0-486-29569-9 (pbk.)
   1. Science fiction, English.   I. Gardner, Martin, 1914–
II. Title.   III. Series.
PR5772.G37   1997
823'.912 — dc21

96-29836
CIP

Manufactured in the United States of America
Dover Publications, Inc., 31 East 2nd Street, Mineola, N.Y. 11501

Contents

Introduction

There is no need to sketch here the life of an author as well known as H. G. Wells (1866–1946). If you care to learn the biographical details, you can find them in encyclopedias, in books about modern British authors, in more than a dozen biographies and in Wells's 1934 autobiography, *Experiment in Autobiography: Discoveries and Conclusions of a Very Ordinary Brain* (*Since 1866*).

As everyone knows, Wells was a prolific writer of novels, short stories and nonfiction. The most complete collection of his short fiction, *The Short Stories of H. G. Wells*, was published in London in 1927. There have since been many less complete anthologies. *The Man with a Nose* (1984), edited by J. R. Hammond, contains nineteen short stories that do not appear in any previous collection.

The book you now hold is a selection of six of the most famous short tales by Wells. I have not included "The Time Machine" and "The Invisible Man" because they are novellas. (Available in Dover Thrift Editions: 28472-7 and 27071-8, respectively.) I have also ignored such well-known stories as "The Man Who Could Work Miracles" because they are closer to fantasy than to science fiction.

I have written an introduction to each story to document its first publication and to make relevant comments. It is interesting to note that among Wells's many realistic stories, almost none is worth remembering.

THE COUNTRY OF THE BLIND

Wells's original version of "The Country of the Blind" was first published in *The Strand Magazine* (May 1904), with eight illustrations. At the story's end Nunez, unwilling to have his eyes removed, tries to climb out of the South American valley into which he had tumbled. "He thought of Medina-saroté, and she had become small and remote." Here is the tale's tragic conclusion:

When sunset came he was no longer climbing, but he was far and high. His clothes were torn, his limbs were blood-stained, he was bruised in many places, but he lay as if he were at his ease, and there was a smile on his face.

From where he rested the valley seemed as if it were in a pit and nearly a mile below. Already it was dim with haze and shadow, though the mountain summits around him were things of light and fire. The mountain summits around him were things of light and fire, and the little things in the rocks near at hand were drenched with light and beauty, a vein of green mineral piercing the grey, a flash of small crystal here and there, a minute, minutely-beautiful orange lichen close beside his face. There were deep, mysterious shadows in the gorge, blue deepening into purple, and purple into a luminous darkness, and overhead was the illimitable vastness of the sky. But he heeded these things no longer, but lay quite still there, smiling as if he were content now merely to have escaped from the valley of the Blind, in which he had thought to be King. And the glow of the sunset passed, and the night came, and still he lay there, under the cold, clear stars.

In 1939 Wells revised his story for a limited edition of 280 copies published by London's Golden Cockerel Press. Although the revised version is almost a short novel — Wells added some three thousand words — I give it here because very few Wells admirers are even aware of its existence. In this book's introduction Wells wrote:

The stress [in the original version] is upon the spiritual isolation of those who see more keenly than their fellows and the tragedy of their incommunicable appreciation of life. The visionary dies, a worthless outcast, finding no

1

other escape from his gift but death, and the blind world goes on, invincibly self-satisfied and secure. But in the later story vision becomes something altogether more tragic; it is no longer a story of disregarded loveliness and release; the visionary sees destruction sweeping down upon the whole blind world he has come to endure and even to love; he sees it plain, and he can do nothing to save it from its fate.

Although both stories are beautifully written and emotionally moving, it is their metaphorical level that elevates them to greatness. Wells must have had in mind Plato's famous allegory of the cave in the seventh book of *The Republic*. Socrates asks Glaucon to imagine the fate of a man who goes outside the cave — a cave where one can see only shadows on a wall — into the great outside world of sunlight. Imagine, Socrates says, that man returning to the cave's darkness:

And if there were a contest, and he had to compete in measuring the shadows with the prisoners who had never moved out of the den, while his sight was still weak, and before his eyes had become steady (and the time which would be needed to acquire this new habit of sight might be very considerable), would he not be ridiculous? Men would say of him that up he went and down he came without his eyes; and that it was better not even to think of ascending; and if any one tried to loose another and lead him up to the light, let them only catch the offender, and they would put him to death.

No question, he said.

This entire allegory, I said, you may now append, dear Glaucon, to the previous argument; the prison-house is the world of sight, the light of the fire is the sun, and you will not misapprehend me if you interpret the journey upwards to be the ascent of the soul into the intellectual world according to my poor belief, which, at your desire, I have expressed — whether rightly or wrongly God knows. But, whether true or false, my opinion is that in the world of knowledge the idea of good appears last of all, and is seen only with an effort; and, when seen, is also inferred to be the universal author of all things beautiful and right, parent of light and of the lord of light in this visible world, and the immediate source of reason and truth in the intellectual; and that this is the power upon which he who would act rationally either in public or private life must have his eye fixed.

I agree, he said, as far as I am able to understand you.

Moreover, I said, you must not wonder that those who attain to this beatific vision are unwilling to descend to human affairs; for their souls are ever hastening into the upper world where they desire to dwell; which desire of theirs is very natural, if our allegory may be trusted.

Yes, very natural.

And is there anything surprising in one who passes from divine contemplations to the evil state of man, misbehaving himself in a ridiculous manner; if, while his eyes are blinking and before he has become accustomed to the surrounding darkness, he is compelled to fight in courts of law, or in other places, about the images or the shadows of images of justice, and is endeavouring to meet the conceptions of those who have never yet seen absolute justice?

Anything but surprising, he replied.

Any one who has common sense will remember that the bewilderments of the eyes are of two kinds, and arise from two causes, either from coming out of the light or from going into the light, which is true of the mind's eye, quite as much as of the bodily eye; and he who remembers this when he sees any one whose vision is perplexed and weak, will not be too ready to laugh; he will first ask whether that soul of man has come out of the brighter life, and is unable to see because unaccustomed to the dark, or having turned from darkness to the day is dazzled by excess of light. And he will count the one happy in his condition and state of being, and he will pity the other; or, if he have a mind to laugh at the soul which comes from below into the light, there will be more reason in this than in the laugh which greets him who returns from above out of the light into the den.

The allegory, as Wells presents it, is a powerful one that applies to all true believers in a fixed ideology, whether political or religious, who are blind to knowledge and reason. Was not the Soviet Union, in the grip of Karl Marx's crank economics, for decades a country of the blind? Were not Soviet leaders of vision executed or banished to Siberia by the blind and cruel Stalin? In post-Stalin Russia hundreds were even confined to mental hospitals in the belief that anyone who opposed the official ideology must be mentally unbalanced!

Was not Hitler's Germany another country of the blind? Is not today's China, still in the grip of obsolete Marxism, another blind country? As in Stalin's Russia, those who see clearly the evils of Chinese totalitarianism are still being killed or imprisoned by blind leaders.

Wells's allegorical tale applies with equal force to dogmatic religions and cults. Extremist Catholics, Jews, Protestants and Moslems, and the unshakable members of a hundred religious cults around the world, do not know they are blind. It is almost impossible to persuade them by argument that there is a wider world of light. "You cannot even fight happily," Nunez reflects, "with creatures that stand upon a different mental basis to yourself."

So persuasive and strong is the rhetoric of the blind that even men and women of vision are often tempted to believe. One thinks of that terrible scene in George Orwell's *Nineteen Eighty-Four* in which Winston, after hours of brainwashing, actually imagines for a fleeting instant that when O'Brien holds up four fingers he sees five — a proof by O'Brien that even mathematical truth is what the Party proclaims. Two plus 2 can equal 5 or 3 depending on what the Party finds expedient.

Nunez, passionately in love with Medina-saroté, comes close to accept-

ing surgery that will deprive him of sight. The blind residents of the val
ley believe that their world is covered by a stone roof above which is the
god they call the Wisdom Above. So impressive are their arguments that
for a moment, like Orwell's Winston, Nunez "almost doubted whether in
deed he was not the victim of hallucination in not seeing it [the lid of
rock] overhead."

We all know persons who, because they are living in a region of the
blind, or are married to a resident of such a region, find it necessary to
adapt, to pretend to believe in the ideology of a loved spouse or of
friends around them. In Wells's first version of his story, Nunez prefer
death by exposure to the loss of his eyes. In the revised version, after dis
covering a mammoth rockslide that will destroy the Country of the Blind
he manages to escape with Medina-saroté before the doom falls.

Although Medina-saroté adjusts well enough to Nunez's world to raise
his children, she never fully escapes from the mind-set of her past. She
does not want to lose her faith in the Wisdom Above. The outside world
may be beautiful, she admits, in the story's poignant ending, but she re
fuses medical help that might give her vision. She still thinks it must be
terrible to see. "If I am dreaming," so goes the old evangelical hymn, "let
me dream on."

❧

THREE hundred miles and more from Chimborazo, one hundred from
the snows of Cotopaxi, in the wildest wastes of Ecuador's Andes, where
the frost-and-sun-rotted rocks rise in vast pinnacles and cliffs above the
snows, there was once a mysterious mountain valley, called the Country o
the Blind. It was a legendary land, and until quite recently people doubted
if it was anything more than a legend. Long years ago, ran the story, that val
ley lay so far open to the world that men, daring the incessant avalanches
might clamber at last through frightful gorges and over an icy pass into its
equable meadows; and thither indeed men went and settled, a family or so
of Peruvian half-breeds fleeing from the lust and tyranny of an evil Spanish
ruler. Then came the stupendous outbreak of Mindobamba, when it was
night in Quito for seventeen days, and the water was boiling at Yaguach
and all the fish floating dying even as far as Guayaquil; everywhere along
the Pacific slopes there were landslips and swift thawings and sudden floods
and one whole side of the old Arauca crest slipped and came down in thun
der, and cut off this Country of the Blind, as it seemed, for ever from the
exploring feet of men.

But, said the story, one of these early settlers had chanced to be on the
hither side of the gorge when the world had so terribly shaken itself, and

perforce he had to forget his wife and his child and all the friends and possessions he declared he had left up there, and begin life again in the lower world.

He had a special reason to account for his return from that fastness, into which he had first been carried lashed to a llama, beside a vast bale of gear, when he was a child. The valley, he said, had in it all that the heart of man could desire — sweet water, pasture, an even climate, slopes of rich brown soil with tangles of a shrub that bore an excellent fruit, and on one side great hanging pine forests that held the avalanches high. Far overhead, a semicircle of ice-capped precipices of grey-green rock brooded over that glowing garden; but the glacier stream flowed away by the farther slopes and only very rarely did an ice-fall reach the lower levels. In this valley it neither rained nor snowed, but the abundant springs gave a rich green pasture, that patient irrigation was spreading over all the valley space. The surplus water gathered at last in a little lake beneath the cirque and vanished with a roar into an unfathomable cavern. The settlers, he said, were doing very well indeed there. Their beasts did well and multiplied, and only one thing marred their happiness. Yet it was enough to mar it greatly; some sinister quality hidden in that sweet and bracing air. A strange disease had come upon them, and had made all the children born to them there — and indeed several older children also — blind. So that the whole valley seemed likely to become a valley of blind men.

It was, he said, to seek some charm or antidote against this plague of blindness that with infinite fatigue, danger and difficulty he had returned down the gorge. In those days, in such cases, men did not think of germs and infections but of sins; and it seemed to him that the reason of this affliction must lie in the negligence of these priestless immigrants to set up a shrine so soon as they entered the valley. He wanted a shrine — a handsome, cheap, effectual shrine — to be set up in the valley; he wanted relics and suchlike potent things of faith, blessed objects and mysterious medals and prayers. In his wallet he had a bar of native silver for which he would not account; he insisted there was none in the valley, with something of the insistence of an inexpert liar. The settlers had all clubbed their money and ornaments together, having little need for such treasure up there, he said, to buy them holy help against their ill. I figure this young mountaineer, sunburnt, gaunt and anxious, hat-brim clutched feverishly, a man all unused to the ways of the lower world, telling this story to some keen-eyed, attentive priest before the great convulsion; I can picture him presently seeking to return with pious and infallible remedies against that trouble, and the infinite dismay with which he must have faced the tumbled and still monstrously crumbling vastness where the gorge had once come out. But the rest of his tale of mischances is lost to me, save that I know he died of punishment in the mines. His offence I do not know.

But the idea of a valley of blind folk had just that appeal to the imagination that a legend requires if it is to live. It stimulates fantasy. It invents its own detail.

And recently this story has been most remarkably confirmed. We know now the whole history of this Country of the Blind from that beginning to its recent and tragic end.

We know now that amidst the little population of that now isolated and forgotten valley the contagion ran its course. Even the older children became groping and purblind, and the young saw but dimly, and the children that were born to them never saw at all. But life was very easy in that snow-rimmed basin, lost to all the world, with neither thorns nor briers, with food upon the bushes in its season, with no evil insects nor any beasts save the gentle breed of llamas they had lugged and thrust and followed up the beds of the shrunken rivers in the gorges by which they had come. The first generation had become purblind so gradually that they scarcely noted their loss. They guided the sightless youngsters who followed them hither and thither until they knew the whole valley marvellously, and when at last sight died out altogether among them the race lived on. They had even time to adapt themselves to the blind control of fire, which they made carefully in stoves of stone. They were a simple strain of people at the first, unlettered, only slightly touched with Spanish civilisation, but with something of a tradition of the arts of old Peru and its lost philosophy. Generation followed generation. They forgot many things; they devised many things. Their tradition of the greater world they came from became mythical in colour and uncertain. In all things save sight they were strong and able; and presently the chances of birth and heredity produced one who had an original mind and who could talk and persuade among them, and then afterwards another. These two passed, leaving their effects, and the little community grew in numbers and understanding, and met and settled all the social and economic problems that arose, sensibly and peaceably. There came a time when a child was born who was fifteen generations from that ancestor who went out of the valley with a bar of silver to seek God's aid, and who never returned. Then it chanced that a man came into this community from the outer world and troubled their minds very greatly. He lived with them for many months, and escaped very narrowly from their final disaster.

He was a mountaineer from the country near Quito, a man who had been down to the sea and had seen the world, and he was taken on by a party of Englishmen under Sir Charles Pointer, who had come out of Ecuador to climb mountains, to replace one of their three Swiss guides who had fallen ill. He climbed here and he climbed there, and then came the attempt on Parascotopetl, the "rotten" mountain, the Matterhorn of the Andes, in which he was lost to the outer world so that he was given up for dead.

Everyone who knew anything of the mountain-craft had warned the little expedition against the treachery of the rocks in this range, but apparently it was not a rock-fall that caught this man Nunez but an exceptional snow-cornice. The party had worked its difficult and almost vertical way up to the very foot of the last and greatest precipice, and had already built itself a night shelter upon a little shelf of rock amidst the snow, when the accident occurred. Suddenly they found that Nunez had disappeared, without a sound. They shouted, and there was no reply; they shouted and whistled, they made a cramped search for him, but their range of movement was very limited. There was no moon, and their electric torches had only a limited range.

As the morning broke they saw the traces of his fall. It seems impossible he could have uttered a cry. The depths had snatched him down. He had slipped eastward towards the unknown side of the mountain; far below he had struck a steep slope of snow, and ploughed his way down it in the midst of a snow avalanche. His track went straight to the edge of a frightful precipice, and beyond that everything was hidden. Far, far below, and hazy with distance, they could see trees rising out of a narrow, shut-in valley — the lost Country of the Blind. But they did not know it was the lost Country of the Blind, nor distinguish it in any way from any other narrow streak of sheltered upland valley. Unnerved by this disaster, they abandoned their attempt in the afternoon, and Pointer, who was financing the attempt, was called away to urgent private business before he could make another attack. To this day Parascotopetl lists an unconquered crest, and Pointer's shelter crumbles unvisited somewhere amidst the snows.

And this man who fell survived.

At the end of the slope he fell a thousand feet, and came down in the midst of a cloud of snow upon a snow slope even steeper than the one above. Down this he was whirled, stunned and insensible, but miraculously without a bone broken in his body; and then the gradients diminished, and at last he rolled out and lay still, buried amidst a softening heap of the white masses that had accompanied him and saved him. He came to himself with a dim fancy that he was ill in bed; then realised his position, worked himself loose and, after a rest or so, out until he saw the stars. He rested flat upon his chest for a space, wondering where he was and what had happened to him. He explored his limbs, they ached exceedingly but they were unbroken. He discovered that several of his buttons were gone and his coat turned over his head. His knife had gone from his pocket and his cap was lost, though it had been tied under his chin. His face was grazed; he was scratched and contused all over. He recalled that he had been looking for loose stones to raise a piece of the shelter wall. His ice-axe had disappeared.

He looked up to see, exaggerated by the ghastly light of the rising moon, the tremendous flight he had taken. For a while he lay, gazing blankly at that vast pale cliff towering above, rising moment by moment out of a subsiding tide of darkness. Since the light struck it first above it seemed to be streaming upward out of nothing. Its phantasmal mysterious beauty held him for space, and then he was seized with a paroxysm of sobbing laughter. . . .

After a great interval of time he became aware that he was near the lower edge of the snow. Below, down what was now a moonlit and practicable slope, he saw the dark and broken appearance of rock-strewn turf. He struggled to his feet, aching in every limb, got down painfully from the heaped loose snow about him, went downward until he was on the turf, and there dropped rather than lay beside a boulder, drank deep from the flask in his inner pocket, and instantly fell asleep. . . .

He was awakened by the singing of birds in trees far below.

He sat up stiffly and perceived he was on a little alp at the foot of a great precipice, grooved by the gulley down which he and his snow had come. Over against him another wall of jagged rock reared itself against the sky. The gorge between these precipices ran east and west and was full of the morning sunlight, which lit to the westward the mass of fallen mountain that had blocked the way to the world. Below him it seemed there was a precipice equally steep, but beyond the snow in the gulley he found a chimney dripping with snow-water down which a desperate man might venture. He found it easier than it looked, and came at last to another desolate alp, and then after a rock climb of no particular difficulty to a steep slope of trees. He took his bearings and turned his face eastward, for he saw it opened out above upon green meadows, among which he now glimpsed quite distinctly a cluster of stone huts of unfamiliar fashion. At times his progress was like clambering along the face of a wall, and after a time the rays of the rising sun were intercepted by a vast bastion, the voices of the singing birds died away, and the air grew cold and dark about him. But the distant valley with its houses seemed all the brighter for that. He presently came to talus, and among the rocks he noted — for he was an observant man — an unfamiliar fern that seemed to clutch out of the crevices with intense green hands. He picked a frond or so and gnawed its stalk and found it helpful. There were bushes but the fruit had not formed upon them.

About midday he emerged from the shadow of the great bluff into the sunlight again. And now he was only a few hundred yards from the valley meadows. He was weary and very stiff; he sat down in the shadow of a rock, filled up his nearly empty flask with water from a spring, drank it down, and rested for a time before he went on towards the houses.

They were very strange to his eyes, and indeed the whole aspect of that valley became, as he regarded it, queerer and more unfamiliar. The greater part of its surface was lush green meadow, starred with many beautiful flowers, irrigated with extraordinary care, and bearing evidence of systematic cropping piece by piece. High up and ringing the valley about was a wall, and what appeared to be a circumferential water-channel, which received the runlets from the snows above and from which little trickles of water had been led to feed the meadows. On the higher slopes above this wall, flocks of llamas cropped the scanty herbage amidst the tangled shrubs. Sheds, apparently shelters or feeding-places for the llamas, stood against the boundary wall here and there. The irrigation streams ran together into a main channel down the centre of the valley, that debouched into a little lake below a semicircle of precipices, and this central canal was enclosed on either side by a wall breast-high. This wall gave a singularly urban quality to this secluded place, a quality that was greatly enhanced by the fact that a number of paths paved with green, grey, black and white stones, and each with a curious little kerb at the side, ran hither and thither in an orderly manner. The houses of the central village were quite unlike the casual and higgledy-piggledy agglomeration of the mountain villages he knew; they stood in a continuous row on either side of a central street of astonishing cleanness; here and there their parti-coloured façade was pierced by a door, and not a solitary window broke their even frontage. They were parti-coloured with extraordinary irregularity; smeared with a sort of plaster that was sometimes grey, sometimes drab, sometimes slate-coloured or dark-brown; and it was the sight of this wild plastering first brought the word "blind" into the thoughts of the explorer. "The good man who did that," he thought, "must have been as blind as a bat."

He descended a steep place and so came to the wall and channel that ran about the valley, near where the latter spouted out its surplus contents into the lake. He could see now a number of men and women resting on piled heaps of grass, as if taking a siesta, in the remoter part of the meadow, and nearer the village a number of recumbent children; and then nearer at hand three men carrying pails on yokes along a little path that ran from the encircling wall towards the houses. These latter were clad in garments of llama cloth and boots and belts of leather, and they wore caps of cloth with back and ear flaps. They followed one another in single file, walking slowly and yawning as they walked, like men who have been up all night. There was something so reassuringly prosperous and respectable in their bearing that after a moment's hesitation Nunez stood forward as conspicuously as possible upon his rock, and gave vent to a mighty shout that evoked a thousand echoes round and about the valley.

The three men stopped and moved their heads as if they were looking about them. They turned their faces this way and that, and Nunez gesticulated with freedom. But they did not appear to see him for all his gestures, and after a time, directing themselves towards the mountain far away to the right, they shouted as if in answer. Nunez bawled again and then once more, and as he gestured ineffectually the word "blind" came once more to the front of his thought. "The fools must be blind," he said.

When at last, after much shouting and irritation, Nunez crossed the stream by a little bridge, came through a gate in the wall, and approached them, he realised that they were indeed blind. He knew already that this was the Country of the Blind of which the legends told. Conviction had sprung upon him, and a sense of great and rather enviable adventure. The three stood side by side, not looking at him, but with their ears directed towards him, judging him by his unfamiliar steps. They stood close together like men a little afraid, and he could see their eyelids closed and shrunken, as if the very balls beneath them had shrunk away. There was an expression near awe on their faces.

"A man," one said, in hardly recognisable Spanish — "a man it is — a man or a beast that walks like a man — coming down from the rocks."

But Nunez advanced with the confident steps of a youth who enters upon life. All the old stories of the lost valley and the Country of the Blind had come back to his mind, and through his thoughts ran this old proverb, as if it were a refrain —

"In the Country of the Blind the One-Eyed Man is King."
"In the Country of the Blind the One-Eyed Man is King."

And very civilly he gave them greeting. He talked to them and used his eyes.

"Where does he come from, brother Pedro?" asked one.

"Down out of the rocks."

"Over the mountains I come," said Nunez, "out of the country beyond there — where men can see. From near Bogota, where there are a hundred thousands of people, and where the city passes out of sight."

"Sight?" muttered Pedro. "Sight?"

"He comes," said the second blind man, "out of the rocks."

The cloth of their coats Nunez saw was curiously fashioned, each with a different sort of stitching.

They startled him by a simultaneous movement towards him, each with a hand outstretched. He stepped back from the advance of these spread fingers.

"Come hither," said the third blind man, following his motion and clutching him neatly.

And they held Nunez and felt him over, saying no word further until they had done so.

"Carefully," he cried, when a finger was poked in his eye, and he realised that they thought that organ, with its fluttering lids, a queer thing in him. They felt over it again.

"A strange creature, Correa," said the one called Pedro. "Feel the coarseness of his hair. Like a llama's hair."

"Rough he is as the rocks that begot him," said Correa, investigating Nunez's unshaven chin with a soft and slightly moist hand. "Perhaps he will grow finer." Nunez struggled a little under their examination, but they gripped him firm.

"Carefully," he said again.

"He speaks," said the third man. "Certainly he is a man."

"Ugh!" said Pedro, at the roughness of his coat.

"And you have come into the world?" asked Pedro.

"*Out* of the world. Over mountains and glaciers; right over above there, half-way to the sun. Out of the great big world that goes down from here, twelve days' journey to the sea."

They scarcely seemed to heed him. "The fathers have told us men may be made by the forces of Nature," said Correa. "It is the warmth of things and moisture, and rottenness — rottenness."

"Let us lead him to the elders," said Pedro.

"Shout first," said Correa, "lest the children be afraid. This is a marvellous occasion."

So they shouted, and Pedro went first and took Nunez by the hand to lead him to the houses.

He drew his hand away. "I can see," he said.

"See?" said Correa.

"Yes, see," said Nunez, turning towards him, and stumbled against Pedro's pail.

"His senses are still imperfect," said the third blind man. "He stumbles, and talks unmeaning words. Lead him by the hand."

"As you will," said Nunez, and was led along smiling.

It seemed they knew nothing of sight.

Well, all in good time, he would teach them.

He heard people shouting, and saw a number of figures gathered together in the middle roadway of the village.

He found it taxed his nerve and patience more than he had anticipated, that first encounter with the population of the Country of the Blind. The place seemed larger as he drew near to it, and the smeared plasterings queerer, and a crowd of children and men and women (the women and girls, he was pleased to note, had some of them quite sweet faces, for all that their eyes were shut and sunken) came about him, and mobbed him, holding on to him, touching him with soft, sensitive hands, smelling at him, and listening for every word he spoke. Some of the maidens and children, however, kept aloof as if afraid, and indeed his voice seemed coarse and rude beside their softer notes. His three guides kept close to him with an effect of proprietorship, and said again and again, "A wild man out of the rocks."

"Bogota," he said. "Bogota. Over the mountain crests."

"A wild man — using wild words," said Pedro. "Did you hear that — *Bogota?* His mind is hardly formed yet. He has only the beginnings of speech."

A little boy nipped his head. "Bogota!" he said mockingly.

"Ay! A city to your village. I come from the great world — where men have eyes and see."

"His name's Bogota," they said.

"He stumbled," said Correa, "stumbled twice as we came hither."

"Bring him to the elders."

And they thrust him suddenly through a doorway into a room as black as pitch, save at the end there faintly glowed a fire. The crowd closed in behind him and shut out all but the faintest glimmer of day, and before he could arrest himself he had fallen headlong over the feet of a seated man. His arm, outflung, struck the face of someone else as he went down; he felt the soft impact of features and heard a cry of anger, and for a moment he struggled against a number of hands that clutched him. It was a one-sided fight. An inkling of the situation came to him, and he lay quiet.

"I fell down," he said, "I couldn't see in this pitchy darkness. Who could?"

There was a pause as if the unseen persons about him tried to understand his words. Then the voice of Correa said: "He is but newly formed. He stumbles as he walks and mingles words that mean nothing with his speech."

Others also said things about him that he heard or understood imperfectly.

"May I sit up?" he asked, in a pause. "I will not struggle against you again."

They consulted and let him rise.

The voice of an older man began to question him, and Nunez found himself trying to explain the great world out of which he had fallen, and the sky and mountains and sight and suchlike marvels, to these elders who sat in darkness in the Country of the Blind. And they would believe and understand nothing whatever he told them, a thing quite outside his expectation. They would not even understand many of his words. For fourteen generations these people had been blind and cut off from all the seeing world; the names for all the things of sight had faded and changed; the story of the outer world was faded and changed to a child's story; and they had ceased to concern themselves with anything beyond the rocky slopes above their circling wall. Blind men of genius had arisen among them and questioned the shreds of belief and tradition they had brought with them from their seeing days, and had dismissed all these things as idle fancies, and replaced them with new and saner explanations. Much of their imagination had shrivelled with their eyes, and they had made for themselves new imaginations with their ever more sensitive ears and finger-tips. Slowly Nunez realised this; that his expectation of wonder and reverence at his origin and his gifts was not to be borne out; and after his poor attempt to explain sight to them had been set aside as the confused version of a new-made being describing the marvels of his incoherent sensations, he subsided, a little dashed, into listening to their instruction.

The eldest of the blind men explained to him life and philosophy and religion, how that the world (meaning their valley) had been first an empty hollow in the rocks and then had come, first, inanimate things without the gift of touch, from these grass and bushes and after that llamas and a few other creatures that had little sense, and then men, and at last angels, whom one could hear singing and making fluttering sounds, but whom none could touch at all, which puzzled Nunez greatly until he thought of the birds.

The elder went on to tell Nunez how "by the Wisdom above us" time had been divided into the warm and the cold, which are the blind equivalents of day and night, and how it was good to sleep in the warm, and work during the cold, so that now, but for his advent, the whole town of the blind would have been asleep. He said Nunez must have been specially created to learn and serve the wisdom they had acquired, and for all his mental incoherency and stumbling behaviour he must have courage, and do his best to learn; and at that all the people in the doorway murmured encouragingly. He said the night — for the blind call their day night — was now far gone, and it behoved everyone to go back to sleep. He asked Nunez if he knew how to sleep, and Nunez said he did, but that before sleep he wanted food.

They brought him food, llama's milk in a bowl, and rough salted bread, and led him into a lonely place to eat out of their hearing, and afterwards to slumber, until the chill of the mountain evening roused them to begin their day again. But Nunez slumbered not at all.

Instead, he sat up in the place where they had left him, resting his limbs and turning the unanticipated circumstances of his arrival over and over in his mind.

Every now and then he laughed, sometimes with amusement and sometimes with indignation.

"Unformed mind!" he said. "Got no senses yet! They little know they've been insulting their heaven-sent king and master. I see I must bring them to reason. Let me think — let me think."

He was still thinking when the sun set.

Nunez had an eye for all beautiful things, and it seemed to him that the glow upon the snowfields and glaciers that rose about the valley on every side was the most beautiful thing he had ever seen. His eyes went from that inaccessible glory to the village and irrigated fields, fast sinking into the twilight, and suddenly a wave of emotion took him, and he thanked God from the bottom of his heart that the power of sight had been given him.

He heard a voice calling to him from out of the house of the elders.

"Ya ho there, Bogota! Come hither!"

At that he stood up smiling. He would show these people once and for all what sight would do for a man. They would seek him but not find him.

"You move not, Bogota," said the voice.

He laughed noiselessly, and made two stealthy steps aside from the path.

"Trample not on the grass, Bogota; that is not allowed."

Nunez had scarcely heard the sound he made himself. He stopped amazed.

The owner of the voice came running up the piebald path towards him.

"Why did you not come when I called you?" said the blind man. "Must you be led like a child? Cannot you hear the path as you walk?"

Nunez laughed. "I can see it," he said.

"There is no such word as *see*," said the blind man after a pause. "Cease this folly and follow the sound of my feet."

Nunez followed, a little annoyed.

"My time will come," he said.

"You'll learn," the blind man answered. "There is much to learn in the world."

"Has no one told you, 'In the Country of the Blind the One-eyed Man is King?' "

"What is blind?" asked the man carelessly over his shoulder.

Four days passed, and the fifth found the King of the Blind still incognito, as a clumsy and useless stranger among his subjects.

It was, he found, much more difficult to proclaim himself than he had supposed, and in the meantime, while he meditated his *coup d'état*, he did what he was told and learned the manners and customs of the Country of the Blind. He found working and going about at night a particularly irksome thing, and he decided that that should be the first thing he would change in his little kingdom.

They led a simple, laborious life, these people, with all the elements of virtue and happiness, as these things can be understood by men. They toiled, but not oppressively; they had food and clothing sufficient for their needs; they had days and seasons of rest; they made much of music and singing, and there was love among them, and little children.

It was marvellous with what confidence and precision they went about their ordered world. Everything, you see, had been made to fit their needs; each of the radiating paths of the valley area had a constant angle to the others, and was distinguished by a special notch upon its kerbing; all obstacles and irregularities of path and meadow had long since been cleared away; all their methods and procedure arose naturally from their special needs. Their senses had become marvellously acute; they could hear and judge the slightest gesture of a man a dozen paces away — could hear the very beating of his heart. Intonation had long replaced expression with them, and touches gesture, and their work with hoe and spade and fork was as free and confident as garden work can be. Their sense of smell was extraordinarily fine; they could distinguish individual differences as readily as a dog can, and they went about the tending of the llamas, who lived among the rocks above and came to the wall for food and shelter, with ease and confidence. It was only when at last Nunez sought to assert himself that he found how easy and confident their movements could be.

He rebelled only after he had tried persuasion.

At first on several occasions he sought to tell them of sight. "Look you here, you people," he said. "There are things you do not understand in me."

Once or twice one or two of them attended to him; they sat with faces downcast and ears turned intelligently towards him though with a faintly ironical smile on their lips, while he did his best to tell them what it was to see. Among his hearers was a girl, with eyes less red and sunken than the others, so that one could almost fancy she was hiding eyes, and she especially he hoped to persuade.

He spoke of the beauties of sight, of watching the mountains, of the sky and the sunrise, and they heard him with amused incredulity that presently became condemnatory. They told him that there were indeed no mountains at all, but that the end of the rocks where the llamas grazed was indeed the end of the world; the rocks became steeper and steeper, became pillars and thence sprang a cavernous roof of the universe, from which the dew and avalanches fell; and when he maintained stoutly the world had neither end nor roof such as they supposed, they were shocked and they said his thoughts were wicked. So far as he could describe sky and clouds and stars to them, his world seemed to them a hideous void, a terrible blankness in the place of the smooth roof to things in which they believed — it was an article of faith with them that above the rocks the cavern roof was exquisitely smooth to the touch. They called it the Wisdom Above.

He saw that in some manner he shocked them by his talk of clouds and stars, and so he gave up that aspect of the matter altogether, and tried to show them the practical value of sight. One morning he saw Pedro in the path called Seventeen and coming towards the central houses, but still too far off for hearing or scent, and he told them as much. "In a little while," he prophesied, "Pedro will be here." An old man remarked that Pedro had no business on Path Seventeen, and then, as if in confirmation, that individual as he drew near turned and went transversely into Path Ten, and so back with nimble paces to the outer wall. They mocked Nunez when Pedro did not arrive, and afterwards, when he asked Pedro questions to clear his character, Pedro denied and outfaced him, and was afterwards hostile to him.

Then he induced them to let him go a long way up the sloping meadows towards the wall with one complacent individual, and to him he promised to describe all that happened among the houses. He noted certain comings and goings, but the things that really seemed to signify to these people happened inside of or behind the windowless houses — the only thing they took note of to test him by — and of these he could see or tell nothing; and it was after the failure of that attempt, and the ridicule they could not repress, that he resorted to force. He thought of seizing a spade and suddenly smiting one or two of them to earth, and so in fair combat showing the advantage of eyes. He went so far with that resolution as to seize his spade, and then he discovered a new thing about himself, and that was that it was impossible for him to hit a blind man in cold blood.

He hesitated and found them all aware that he had snatched up the spade. They stood alert, with their heads on one side, and bent ears towards him for what he would do next.

"Put that spade down," said one, and he felt a sort of helpless horror. He came near obedience.

Then he thrust one backwards against a house wall, and fled past him and out of the village.

He went athwart one of their meadows, leaving a track of trampled grass behind his feet, and presently sat down by the side of one of their ways. He felt something of the buoyancy that comes to all men in the beginning of a fight, but more perplexity. He began to realise that you cannot even fight happily with creatures that stand upon a different mental basis to yourself. Far away he saw a number of men carrying spades and sticks come out of the street of houses, and advance in a spreading line along the several paths towards him. They advanced slowly, speaking frequently to one another, and ever and again the whole cordon would halt and snuff the air and listen.

The first time they did this Nunez laughed. But afterwards he did not laugh.

One struck his trail in the meadow grass, and came stooping and feeling his way along it.

For five minutes he watched the slow extension of the cordon, and then his vague disposition to do something forthwith became frantic. He stood up, went a pace or so towards the circumferential wall, turned, and went back a little way. There they all stood in a crescent, still and listening.

He also stood still, gripping his spade very tightly in both hands. Should he charge them?

The pulse in his ears rang into the rhythm of "In the Country of the Blind the One-eyed Man is King!"

Should he charge them?

He looked back at the high and unclimbable wall behind — unclimbable because of its smooth plastering, but withal pierced by many little doors, and at the approaching line of seekers. Behind these, others were now coming out of the street of houses.

Should he charge them?

"Bogota!" called one. "Bogota! where are you!"

He gripped his spade still tighter and advanced down the meadows towards the place of habitations, and directly he moved they converged upon him. "I'll hit them if they touch me," he swore; "by Heaven I will. I'll hit." He called aloud, "Look here, I'm going to do what I like in this valley. Do you hear? I'm going to do what I like and go where I like!"

They were moving in upon him quickly, groping, yet moving rapidly. It was like playing blind man's buff, with everyone blindfolded except one. "Get hold of him!" cried one. He found himself in the arc of a loose curve of pursuers. He felt suddenly he must be active and resolute.

"You don't understand," he cried in a voice that was meant to be great and resolute, and which broke. "You are blind, and I can see. Leave me alone!"

"Bogota! Put down that spade, and come off the grass!"

The last order, grotesque in its urban familiarity, produced a gust of anger.

"I'll hurt you," he said, sobbing with emotion. "By Heaven, I'll hurt you. Leave me alone!"

He began to run, not knowing clearly where to run. He ran from the nearest blind man, because it was a horror to hit him. He stopped, and made a dash to escape from their closing ranks. He made for where a gap was wide, and the men on either side, with a quick perception of the approach of his paces, rushed in on one another. He sprang forward, and then saw he must be caught, and swish! the spade had struck. He felt the soft thud of hand and arm, and the man was down with a yell of pain, and he was through.

Through! And then he was close to the street of houses again, and blind men, whirling spades and stakes, were running with a sort of reasoned swiftness hither and thither.

He heard steps behind him just in time, and found a tall man rushing forward and swiping at the sound of him. He lost his nerve, hurled his spade a yard wide at his antagonist, and whirled about and fled, fairly yelling as he dodged another.

He was panic-stricken. He ran furiously to and fro, dodging when there was no need to dodge, and in his anxiety to see on every side of him at once, stumbling. For a moment he was down and they heard his fall. Far away in the circumferential wall a little doorway looked like Heaven, and he set off in a wild rush for it. He did not even look round at his pursuers until it was gained, and he had stumbled across the bridge, clambered a little way among the rocks, to the surprise and dismay of a young llama, who went leaping out of sight, and lay down sobbing for breath.

And so his *coup d'état* came to an end.

He stayed outside the wall of the Valley of the Blind for two nights and days without food or shelter, and meditated upon the unexpected. There were bushes, but the food on them was not ripe and hard and bitter. It weakened him to eat it. It lowered his courage. During these prowlings he repeated very frequently and always with a profounder note of derision that exploded proverb: "In the Country of the Blind the One-eyed Man is King." He thought chiefly of ways of fighting and conquering these people, and it grew clear that for him no practicable way was possible. He had no weapons, and now it would be hard to get one.

The canker of civilisation had got to him even in Bogota, and he could not find it in himself to go down and assassinate a blind man. Of course, if he did that, he might then dictate terms on the threat of assassinating them all. If he could get near enough to them, that is. And — sooner or later he must sleep! . . .

He tried also to find food among the pine trees, to be comfortable under pine boughs while the frost fell at night and — with less confidence — to catch a llama by artifice in order to try to kill it — perhaps by hammering it with a stone — and so finally, perhaps, to eat some of it. But the llamas had their doubts of him and regarded him with distrustful brown eyes, and spat when he drew near. Fear came on him the second day, an intense fatigue, and fits of shivering. Finally he crawled down to the wall of the Country of the Blind and tried to make terms. He crawled along by the stream shouting, until two blind men came out to the gate and talked to him.

"I was mad," he said. "But I was only newly made."

They said that was better.

He told them he was wiser now, and that he repented of all he had done.

Then he wept without intention, for he was very weak and ill, and they took that as a favourable sign.

They asked him if he still thought he could "*see*."

"No," he said, "that was folly. The word means nothing — less than nothing!"

They asked him what was overhead.

"About ten times the height of a man there is a roof above the world — of rock and wisdom and very, very smooth." . . .

He burst again into hysterical tears. "Before you ask me any more, give me some food or I shall die."

He expected dire punishments, but these blind people showed themselves capable of great toleration. They regarded his rebellion as but one more proof of his general idiocy and inferiority; and after they had whipped him they appointed him to do the simplest and heaviest work they had for anyone to do, and he, seeing no other way of living, did submissively what he was told.

He was ill for some days and they nursed him kindly. That refined his submission. But they insisted on his lying in the dark and that was a great misery. And the chief elders came and talked to him of the wicked levity of his mind, and reproved him so impressively for his doubts about the lid of rock that covered their cosmic casserole that he almost doubted whether indeed he was not the victim of hallucination in not seeing it overhead.

So Nunez humbled himself and became a common citizen of the Country of the Blind, and these people ceased to be a generalised people and became individualities and familiar to him, while the world beyond the mountains became more and more remote and unreal. There was Yacob, his master, a kindly man when not annoyed; there was Pedro, Yacob's nephew; and there was Medina-saroté, who was the youngest daughter of Yacob. She was little esteemed in the world of the blind, because she had a clear-cut face, and lacked the satisfying, glossy smoothness that is the blind man's ideal of feminine beauty; but Nunez thought her beautiful at first, and presently the most beautiful thing in the whole creation. Her closed eyelids were not sunken and red after the common way of the valley, but lay as though they might open again at any moment; and she had eyelashes, which were considered a grave disfigurement. And her voice was strong,

and did not satisfy the acute hearing of the valley swains. So that she had n
lover.

There came a time when Nunez thought that, could he win her, he woul
be resigned to live in the valley for all the rest of his days.

He watched her; he sought opportunities of doing her little services, an
presently he found that she observed him. Once at a rest-day gathering the
sat side by side in the dim starlight, and the music was sweet. His han
came upon hers and he dared to clasp it. Then very tenderly she returne
his pressure. And one day, as they were at their meal in the darkness, he fe
her hand very softly seeking him, and as it chanced the fire leaped then an
he saw the tenderness of her face.

He sought to speak to her.

He went to her one day when she was sitting in the summer moonligh
spinning. The light made her a thing of silver and mystery. He sat down a
her feet and told her he loved her, and told her how beautiful she seeme
to him. He had a lover's voice, he spoke with a tender reverence that cam
near to awe, and she had never before been touched by adoration. She mad
him no definite answer, but it was clear his words pleased her.

After that he talked to her whenever he could take an opportunity. Th
valley became the world for him, and the world beyond the mountain
where men worked and went about in sunlight seemed no more than a fair
tale he would some day pour into her ears. Very tentatively and timidly h
spoke to her of sight.

At first this sight seemed to her the most poetical of fancies, and sh
listened to his description of the stars and the mountains and her own swee
white-lit beauty as though it was a guilty indulgence. She did not believe
she could only half understand, but she was mysteriously delighted, and
seemed to him that she completely understood.

His love lost its awe and took courage. Presently he was for demandin
her of Yacob and the elders in marriage, but she became fearful and delayec
And it was one of her sisters who first told Yacob that Medina-saroté an
Nunez were in love.

From the first there was very great opposition to the marriage of Nune
and Medina-saroté; not so much because they valued her as because the
held him as a being apart, an idiot, incompetent thing, below the permissibl
level of a man. Her sisters opposed it bitterly as bringing discredit on ther
all; and old Yacob, though he had formed a sort of liking for his clumsy
obedient serf, shook his head and said the thing could not be. The youn
men were all angry at the thought of corrupting the race, and one went s
far as to revile and strike Nunez. He struck back. Then for the first time h
found an advantage in seeing, even by twilight, and after that fight no on

was disposed to lift a hand against him. But they still found his marriage impossible.

Old Yacob had a tenderness for his last little daughter, and was grieved to have her weep upon his shoulder.

"You see, my dear, he's an idiot! He has delusions; he can't do anything right."

"I know," wept Medina-saroté. "But he's better than he was. He's getting better. And he's strong, dear father, and kind — stronger and kinder than any other man in the world. And he loves me — and, father, I love him."

Old Yacob was greatly distressed to find her inconsolable, and, besides — what made it more distressing — he liked Nunez for many things. So he went and sat in the windowless council-chamber with the other elders, observing the trend of their talk, and said, at the proper time, "He's better than he was. Very likely, some day, we shall find him as sane as ourselves."

Then afterwards one of the elders, who thought deeply, had an idea. He was the great doctor among these people, their medicine man, and he had a very philosophical and inventive mind, and the idea of curing Nunez of his peculiarities appealed to him. One day when Yacob was present he turned to the topic of Nunez.

"I have examined Bogota," he said, "and the case is clearer to me. I think very probably he might be cured."

"That is what I have always hoped," said old Yacob.

"His brain is affected," said the blind doctor.

The elders murmured assent.

"Now, *what* affects it?"

"Ah!" said old Yacob.

"This," said the doctor, answering his own question. "Those queer things that are called the eyes, and which exist to make an agreeable soft depression in the face, are diseased, in the case of Bogota, in such a way as to affect his brain. They are greatly distended, he has eyelashes, and his eyelids move, and consequently his brain is in a state of constant irritation and distraction."

"Yes?" said old Yacob. "Yes?"

"And I think I may say with reasonable certainty that, in order to cure him completely, all that we need to do is a simple and easy surgical operation — namely, to remove those irritating bodies."

"And then he will be sane?"

"Then he will be perfectly sane, and a quite admirable citizen."

"Thank Heaven for the Wisdom beneath it!" said old Yacob, and went forth at once to tell Nunez of his happy hopes.

But Nunez's manner of receiving the good news struck him as being cold and disappointing.

"One might think," he said, "from the tone you take, that you did not care for my daughter."

It was Medina-saroté who persuaded Nunez to face the blind surgeons.

"*You* do not want me," he said, "to lose my gift of sight?"

She shook her head.

"My world is sight."

Her head dropped lower.

"There are beautiful things, the beautiful little things — the flowers, the lichens among the rocks, the lightness and visible softness on a piece of fur, the far sky with its drifting down of clouds, the sunsets and the stars. And there is *you*. For you alone it is good to have sight, to see your sweet, serene face, your kindly lips, your dear, dear, beautiful hands folded together. . . . It is these eyes of mine you won, these eyes that hold me to you, that these idiots seek. Instead, I must touch you, hear you, and never see you again. I must come under that roof of rock and stone and darkness, that horrible roof under which your imagination stoops. . . . No, you would not have me do that?"

She shuddered to hear him speak of the Wisdom Above in such terms. Her hands went to her ears.

A disagreeable doubt had arisen in him. He stopped, and left the thing a question.

"I wish," she said, "sometimes —" She paused.

"Yes?" said he, a little apprehensively.

"I wish sometimes — you would not talk like that."

"Like what?"

"It's your imagination. I love much of it, but not when you speak of the Wisdom Above. When you talked of those flowers and stars it was different. But now —"

He felt cold. "*Now?*" he said faintly.

She sat quite still.

"You mean — you think — I should be better, better, perhaps —"

He was realising things very swiftly. He felt anger, indeed, anger at the dull course of fate, but also sympathy for her lack of understanding — a sympathy near akin to pity.

"*Dear*," he said, and he could see by her whiteness how intensely her spirit pressed against the things she could not say. He put his arms about her, and kissed her ear, and they sat for a time in silence.

"If I were to consent to this?" he whispered at last, in a voice that was very gentle.

She flung her arms about him weeping wildly. "Oh, if you would," she sobbed, "if only you would!"

"And you have no doubt?"

"Dear heart!" she answered, and pressed his hands with all her strength.

"They will hurt you but little," she said; "and you would be going through this pain — you are going through it, dear lover, for *me*. . . . Dear; if a woman's heart and life can do it, I will repay you. My dearest one, my dearest with that rough, gentle voice, I will repay."

"So be it," he said.

And in silence he turned away from her. For the time he could sit by her no longer.

She could hear his slow retreating footsteps, and something in the rhythm of them threw her into a passion of weeping. . . .

He meant to go to a lonely place where the meadows were beautiful with white narcissus, but as he went he lifted up his eyes and saw the morning, the morning like an angel in golden armour, marching down the steeps. . . .

It seemed to him that before this splendour he, and this blind world in the valley, and his love, and all, were no better than the darkness of an anthill.

He did not turn aside to the narcissus fields as he had meant to do. Instead he went on, and passed through the wall of the circumference and out upon the rocks, and his eyes were always upon the sunlit ice and snow above.

He saw their infinite beauty, and his imagination soared over them to the things he would see no more.

He thought of that great free visible world he was to renounce for ever; the world that was his own, and beyond these encircling mountains; and he had a vision of those further slopes, distance beyond distance, with Bogota, a place of multitudinous stirring beauty, a glory by day, a luminous mystery by night, a place of palaces and fountains and statues and white houses, lying beautifully in the middle distance. He thought how for a day or so one might come down through passes, drawing ever nearer and nearer to its busy streets and ways. He thought of the river journey to follow, from great Bogota to the still vaster world beyond, through towns and villages, forest and desert places, the rushing river day by day, until its banks receded and the big steamers came splashing by, and one had reached the sea — the limitless sea, with its thousand islands, its thousands of islands, and its ships seen dimly far away in their incessant journeyings round and about the greater world. And there, unpent by mountains, one saw the sky — the sky, not such a disc as one saw it here, but a great arch of immeasurable blue, the blue of deeps in which the circling stars were floating.

His eyes scrutinised the imprisoning mountains with a keener enquiry.

It occurred to him that for many days now he had not looked at the cliffs and snow-slopes and gulleys by which he had slid and fallen and clambered down into the valley. He looked now; he looked but he could not find. Something had happened. Something had occurred to change and obliterate the familiar landmarks of his descent. He could not believe it; he rubbed his eyes and looked again. Perhaps he was forgetting. Some fresh fall of snow might have altered the lines and shapes of the exposed surfaces.

In another place too there had been slopes that he had studied very intently. For at times the thought of escape had been very urgent with him. Had they too changed? Had his memory begun to play tricks with him? In one place high up, five hundred feet or so, he had marked a great vein of green crystal that made a sort of slanting way upwards — but alas! died out to nothing. One might clamber to it, but above that there seemed no hope. That was still as it had been. But elsewhere?

Suddenly he stood up with a faint cry of horror in his throat.

"*No!*" he whispered crouching slightly. "No. It was there before!"

But he knew it had not been there before.

It was a long narrow scar of newly exposed rock running obliquely across the face of the precipice at its vastest. Above it and below it was weathered rock. He still struggled against that conviction. But there it was plain and undeniable and *raw*. There could be little doubt of the significance of that fresh scar. An enormous mass of that stupendous mountain wall had slipped. It had shifted a few feet forward and it was being held up for a time, by some inequality of the sustaining rocks. Maybe that would hold it now, but of the shift there was no doubt whatever. Could it settle down again in its new position? He could not tell. He scanned the distant surfaces. Above he saw little white threads of water from the snowfields pouring into this new-made crack. Below, water was already spouting freshly at a dozen points from the lower edge of the loosened mass. And then he saw that other, lesser fissures had also appeared in the mountain wall.

The more he studied that vast rock face the more he realised the possible urgency of its menace. If this movement continued the valley was doomed. He forgot his personal distress in a huge solicitude for this little community of which he had become a citizen. What ought these people to do? What could they do? Abandon their threatened houses? Make new ones on the slopes behind him? And how could he induce them to do it?

Suppose that lap of rock upon which the mass now rested *gave!*

The mountain would fall — he traced the possible fall with his extended hands — so and so and so. It would fall into and beyond the lake. It would bury the lower houses. It might bury the whole village. It might spell destruction for every living thing in the valley. Something they ought to do. Prepare refuges? Organise a possible evacuation? Set him to watch the mountains day by day? But how to make them understand?

If he went down now, very simply, very meekly, without excitement, speaking in low tones and abasing himself before them. If he said: "I am a foolish creature. I am a disgusting creature. I am unfit to touch the hem of the garment of the very least of your wise men. But for once, I pray you, believe in my vision! Believe in my vision! Sometimes such an idiot as I can *see*. Let me have some more tests about this seeing. Because indeed, indeed, I know of a great danger and I can help you to sustain it." . . .

But how could he convince them? What proofs could he give them? After his earlier failures. Suppose he went down now, with his warning fresh in his mind. Suppose he *insisted*.

"Vision. Sight." The mere words would be an outrage to them. They might not let him speak at all. And even then if he was permitted to speak, already it might be too late. At the best it would only set them discussing his case afresh. Almost certainly he would anger them, for how could he tell his tale and not question the Wisdom Above. They might take him and end the recurrent nuisance of him by putting out his eyes forthwith, and the only result of his intervention would be that he would be nursing his bloody eye sockets when the disaster fell. The mountain might hold for weeks and months yet, but again it might not wait at all. Even now it might be creeping. Even now the heat of the day must be expanding those sullen vast masses, thawing the night ice that held them together. Even now the trickling snow-water was lubricating the widening fissures.

Suddenly he saw, he saw plainly, a new crack leap across a shining green mass, and then across the valley came the sound of it like the shot of a gun that starts a race. The mass was moving *now!* There was no more time to waste. No more time for pleas and plans. "Stop!" he cried. "Stop!" and put out his hands as if to thrust back that slow deliberate catastrophe. It is preposterous but he believes he said, "Wait one minute!"

He ran headlong to the little bridge and the gate and rushed down towards the houses, waving his arms and shouting. "The mountain is falling," he screamed. "The whole mountain is falling upon you all. Medina-saroté! Medina-saroté!"

He clattered to the house of old Yacob and burst in upon the sleepers. He shook them and shouted at them, going from one to the other.

"He's gone mad again," they cried aghast at him and even Medina-saroté cowered away from his excitement.

"Come," he said. "Come. Even now it is falling. The mountain is falling."

And he seized her wrist in a grip of steel. "Come!" he cried so masterfully that in terror she obeyed him.

But outside the house there was a crowd that his shouts and noise had awakened, and a score of men had run out already and assembled outside the house and stood in his way.

"Let me pass," he cried. "Let me pass. And come with me — up the further slopes there before it is too late."

"This is too much. This is the last blasphemy," shrieked one of the elders. "Seize him. Hold him!"

"I tell you the mountain is falling. It is coming down upon you even now as you hold me here."

"The Wisdom Above us that loves and protects us *cannot* fall."

"Listen. That rumbling?"

"There has been rumbling like that before. The Wisdom is warning us. It is because of your blasphemies."

"And the ground rocking?"

"Brothers, cast him out! Cast him out of the valley. We have been foolish to harbour him so long. His sin is more than our Providence can endure."

"But I tell you the rocks are falling. The whole mountain is coming down. Listen and you can hear the crashing and the rending of them."

He was aware of a loud hoarse voice intoning through the uproar and drowning his own. "The Wisdom Above loves us. It protects us from all harm. No evil can touch us while the Wisdom is over us. Cast him forth! Cast him forth. Let him take our sins upon him and go!" "Out you go, Bogota," cried a chorus of voices. "Out you go."

"Medina-saroté! Come with me. Come out of this place!"

Pedro threw protective arms about his cousin.

"Medina-saroté!" cried Nunez. "Medina-saroté!"

They pushed him, struggling fiercely, up the path towards the boundaries. They showed all the cruelty now of frightened men. For the gathering noise of the advancing rocks dismayed them all. They wanted to out-do each other in repudiating him. They beat at his face with their fists and kicked his shins and ankles and feet. One or two jabbed at him with knives. He could not see Medina-saroté any longer and he could not see the shifting cliffs because of the blows and because of the blood that poured from a cut on his forehead, but the voices about him seemed to fade as the rumbling clatter of falling fragments wove together and rose into a thunderous roar. He shouted weeping for Medina-saroté to escape as they drove him before them.

They thrust him through a little door and flung him out on to a stony slope with a deliberate violence that sent a flock of llamas helter-skelter. He lay like a cast clout. "And there you stay — and starve," said one. "You and your — *seeing*."

He lifted his head for a last reply.

"I tell you. You will be dead before I am."

"You *fool!*" said the one he had fought, and came back to kick him again and again. "Will you never learn reason?" But he turned hastily to join his fellows when Nunez struggled clumsily to his feet.

He stood swaying like a drunken man.

He had no strength in his limbs. He did his best to wipe the blood from his eyes. He looked at the impending mountain-fall, he looked for a high rocky ledge he had noted that morning and then he turned a despairful face to the encircling doom of the valley. But he did not attempt to climb any further away.

"What's the good of going alone?" he said. "Even if I could. I shall only starve up there."

And then suddenly he saw Medina-saroté seeking him. She emerged from the little door and she was calling his name. In some manner she had contrived to slip away and come to search for him. "Bogota my darling!" she cried. "What have they done to you? Oh *what* have they *done* to you?"

He staggered to meet her, calling her name over and over again.

In another moment her hands were upon his face and she was wiping away the blood and searching softly and skilfully for his cuts and bruises.

"You must stay here now," she panted. "You must stay here for a time. Until you repent. Until you learn to repent. Why did you behave so madly? Why did you say those horrible blasphemies? You don't know you say them, but how are they to tell that? If you come back now they will certainly kill you. I will bring you food. Stay here."

"Neither of us can stay here. *Look!*"

She drew the air in sharply between her teeth at that horrible word "look" which showed that his madness was still upon him.

"There! That thunder!"

"What is it?"

"A stream of rocks are pouring down by the meadows and it is only the beginning of them. *Look* at them. Listen anyhow to the drumming and beating of them! What do you think those sounds mean? *That* and that! Stones! They are bouncing and dancing across the lower meadows by the lake and the waters of the lake are brimming over and rising up to the further houses. Come my darling. Come! Do not question, but come!"

She stood hesitating for a moment. There was a frightful menace now in the storm of sounds that filled the air. Then she crept into his arms. "I am afraid," she said.

He drew her to him and with a renewal of strength began to climb, guiding her feet. His blood smeared her face but there was no time to remedy that. At first she dragged upon him and then, perceiving the strain she caused, she helped and supported him. She was sobbing but also she obeyed.

He concentrated himself now upon reaching that distant shelf, but presently he had to halt for breath, and then only was he free to look back across the valley.

He saw that the foot of the cliff was sliding now down into the lake, scooping its waters before it towards the remoter houses, and that the cascade of rocks was now swifter and greater. They drove over the ground in leaps and bounds with a frightful suggestion in their movements as though they were hunting victims. They were smashing down trees and bushes and demolishing walls and buildings, and still the main bulk of the creeping mountain, deprived now of its supports, had to gather momentum and fall. It was breaking up as it came down. And now little figures appeared from the houses and ran hither and thither. . . .

For the first time Nunez was glad that Medina-saroté was blind.

"Climb! my darling," he said. "Climb!"

"I do not understand."

"Climb!"

A rush of terrified llamas came crowding up past them.

"It is so steep, so steep here. Why are these creatures coming with us?"

"Because they understand. Because they know we are with them. Push through them. Climb."

With an effect of extreme deliberation that mountain-side hung over the doomed valley. For some tense instants Nunez did not hear a sound. His whole being was concentrated in his eyes. Then came the fall and then a stunning concussion that struck his chest a giant's blow. Medina-saroté was flung against the rocks and clung to them with clawing hands. Nunez had an instant's impression of a sea of rocks and earth and fragments of paths and walls and houses, pouring in a swift flood towards him. A spray of wind-driven water bedewed him; they were pelted with mud and broken rock fragments, the wave of debris surged and receded a little and abruptly became still, and then colossal pillars of mist and dust rose up solemnly and deliberately and mounted towering overhead and unfolded and rolled together about them until they were in an impenetrable stinging fog. Silence fell again upon the world and the Valley of the Blind was hidden from him for evermore.

Pallid to the centres of their souls, these two survivors climbed slowly to the crystalline ridge and crouched upon it.

And when some hour or so later that swirling veil of mist and dust had grown thinner and they could venture to move and plan what they would do, Nunez saw through a rent in it far away across a wilderness of tumbled broken rock and in a V-shaped cleft of the broken mountains, the green rolling masses of the foothills, and far beyond them one shining glimpse of the ocean.

Two days later he and Medina-saroté were found by two hunters who had come to explore the scene of this disaster. They were trying to clamber down to the outer world and they were on the verge of exhaustion. They had lived upon water, fern roots and a few berries. They collapsed completely when the hunters hailed them.

They lived to tell their tale, and to settle in Quito among Nunez's people. There he is still living. He is a prosperous tradesman and plainly a very honest man. She is a sweet and gentle lady, her basketwork and her embroidery are marvellous, though of course she makes no use of colour, and she speaks Spanish with an old-fashioned accent very pleasant to the ear.

Greatly daring, I think, they have had four children and they are as stout and sturdy as their father and they can see.

He will talk about his experience when the mood is on him but she says very little. One day however when she was sitting with my wife while Nunez and I were away, she talked a little of her childhood in the valley and of the simple faith and happiness of her upbringing. She spoke of it with manifest regret. It had been a life of gentle routines, free from all complications.

It was plain she loved her children and it was plain she found them and much of the comings and goings about her difficult to understand. She had never been able to love and protect them as she had once loved and protected Nunez.

My wife ventured on a question she had long wanted to ask. "You have never consulted oculists," she began.

"Never," said Medina-saroté. "I have never wanted to *see*."

"But colour — and form and distance!"

"I have no use for your colours and your stars," said Medina-saroté. "I do not want to lose my faith in the Wisdom Above."

"But after all that has happened! Don't you want to see Nunez; see what he is like?"

"But I know what he is like and seeing him might put us apart. He would not be so near to me. The loveliness of *your* world is a complicated and fearful loveliness and mine is simple and near. I had rather Nunez saw for me — because he knows nothing of fear."

"But the *beauty!*" cried my wife.

"It may be beautiful," said Medina-saroté, "but it must be very terrible to *see*."

THE STAR

Many science-fiction novels and stories concern catastrophes that would befall the earth if it were ever struck, or narrowly missed, by a giant comet, asteroid or some other huge celestial object. Wells himself devoted an entire novel, *In the Days of the Comet,* to such an event. However, no short story has ever described what might happen with such riveting vividness as Wells's "The Star."

Strictly speaking, the object is not a star but a dark sister planet beyond the orbit of Neptune. (Pluto had not been discovered when Wells wrote.) For some reason the planet has been shifted from its orbit and is headed toward the sun. On its way it collides with Neptune. The two coalesce to form an incandescent "star" that passes extremely close to the earth before it strikes the sun.

The story is timely. In recent years there has been much speculation about the possibility of a large asteroid hitting the earth — there have been several fairly close encounters — and what steps could be taken to avert the earth's destruction.

In his last paragraph Wells introduces Martian astronomers who watch the star's near collision with our planet. Were he alive today, Wells would probably put his astronomers on Titan. This giant moon of Saturn — it is larger than Mercury — is the only satellite in the solar system with an atmosphere that just might harbor, but probably does not, intelligent life.

"The Star" first appeared in the 1897 Christmas number of London's *The Graphic*. A full-page full-color illustration showed a street packed with Londoners staring at the sky and shouting "It is brighter!" A newsboy holds a sheet with huge red letters that say "Total Destruction of the Earth."

❧

IT was on the first day of the new year that the announcement was made, almost simultaneously from three observatories, that the motion of the planet Neptune, the outermost of all the planets that wheel about the sun, had become very erratic. Ogilvy had already called attention to a suspected retardation in its velocity in December. Such a piece of news was scarcely calculated to interest a world the greater portion of whose inhabitants were unaware of the existence of the planet Neptune, nor outside the astronomical profession did the subsequent discovery of a faint remote speck of light in the region of the perturbed planet cause any very great excitement. Scientific people, however, found the intelligence remarkable enough, even before it became known that the new body was rapidly growing larger and brighter, that its motion was quite different from the orderly progress of the planets, and that the deflection of Neptune and its satellite was becoming now of an unprecedented kind.

Few people without a training in science can realise the huge isolation of the solar system. The sun with its specks of planets, its dust of planetoids, and its impalpable comets, swims in a vacant immensity that almost defeats the imagination. Beyond the orbit of Neptune there is space, vacant so far as human observation has penetrated, without warmth or light or sound, blank emptiness, for twenty million times a million miles. That is the smallest estimate of the distance to be traversed before the very nearest of the stars is attained. And, saving a few comets more unsubstantial than the thinnest flame, no matter had ever to human knowledge crossed this gulf of space, until early in the twentieth century this strange wanderer appeared. A vast mass of matter it was, bulky, heavy, rushing without warning out of the black mystery of the sky into the radiance of the sun. By the second day it was clearly visible to any decent instrument, as a speck with a barely sensible diameter, in the constellation Leo near Regulus. In a little while an opera glass could attain it.

On the third day of the new year the newspaper readers of two hemispheres were made aware for the first time of the real importance of this unusual apparition in the heavens. "A Planetary Collision," one London paper headed the news, and proclaimed Duchaine's opinion that this strange new planet would probably collide with Neptune. The leader writers enlarged upon the topic. So that in most of the capitals of the world, on January 3rd, there was an expectation, however vague, of some imminent phenomenon in the sky; and as the night followed the sunset round the globe, thousands of men turned their eyes skyward to see — the old familiar stars just as they had always been.

Until it was dawn in London and Pollux setting and the stars overhead grown pale. The Winter's dawn it was, a sickly filtering accumulation of daylight, and the light of gas and candles shone yellow in the windows to show where people were astir. But the yawning policeman saw the thing, the busy crowds in the markets stopped agape, workmen going to their work betimes, milkmen, the drivers of newscarts, dissipation going home jaded and pale, homeless wanderers, sentinels on their beats, and in the country, labourers trudging afield, poachers slinking home, all over the dusky quickening country it could be seen — and out at sea by seamen watching for the day — a great white star, come suddenly into the westward sky!

Brighter it was than any star in our skies; brighter than the evening star at its brightest. It still glowed out white and large, no mere twinkling spot of light, but a small round clear shining disc, an hour after the day had come. And where science has not reached, men stared and feared, telling one another of the wars and pestilences that are foreshadowed by these fiery signs in the Heavens. Sturdy Boers, dusky Hottentots, Gold Coast Negroes, Frenchmen, Spaniards, Portuguese, stood in the warmth of the sunrise watching the setting of this strange new star.

And in a hundred observatories there had been suppressed excitement, rising almost to shouting pitch, as the two remote bodies had rushed together, and a hurrying to and fro, to gather photographic apparatus and spectroscope, and this appliance and that, to record this novel astonishing sight, the destruction of a world. For it was a world, a sister planet of our earth, far greater than our earth indeed, that had so suddenly flashed into flaming death. Neptune it was, had been struck, fairly and squarely, by the strange planet from outer space and the heat of the concussion had incontinently turned two solid globes into one vast mass of incandescence. Round the world that day, two hours before the dawn, went the pallid great white star, fading only as it sank westward and the sun mounted above it. Everywhere men marvelled at it, but of all those who saw it none could have marvelled more than those sailors, habitual watchers of the stars, who far away at sea had heard nothing of its advent and saw it now rise like a pigmy moon and climb zenithward and hang overhead and sink westward with the passing of the night.

And when next it rose over Europe everywhere were crowds of watchers on hilly slopes, on house-roofs, in open spaces, staring eastward for the rising of the great new star. It rose with a white glow in front of it, like the glare of a white fire, and those who had seen it come into existence the night before cried out at the sight of it. "It is larger," they cried. "It is brighter!" And, indeed the moon a quarter full and sinking in the west was in its apparent size beyond comparison, but scarcely in all its breadth had it as much brightness now as the little circle of the strange new star.

"It is brighter!" cried the people clustering in the streets. But in the dim observatories the watchers held their breath and peered at one another. "*It is nearer*," they said. "*Nearer!*"

And voice after voice repeated, "It is nearer," and the clicking telegraph took that up, and it trembled along telephone wires, and in a thousand cities grimy compositors fingered the type. "It is nearer." Men writing in offices, struck with a strange realisation, flung down their pens, men talking in a thousand places suddenly came upon a grotesque possibility in those words, "It is nearer." It hurried along awakening streets, it was shouted down the frost-stilled ways of quiet villages; men who had read these things from the throbbing tape stood in yellow-lit doorways shouting the news to the passers-by. "It is nearer." Pretty women, flushed and glittering, heard the news told jestingly between the dances, and feigned an intelligent interest they did not feel. "Nearer! Indeed. How curious! How very, very clever people must be to find out things like that!"

Lonely tramps faring through the wintry night murmured those words to comfort themselves — looking skyward. "It has need to be nearer, for the night's as cold as charity. Don't seem much warmth from it if it *is* nearer, all the same."

"What is a new star to me?" cried the weeping woman kneeling beside her dead.

The schoolboy, rising early for his examination work, puzzled it out for himself — with the great white star, shining broad and bright through the frost-flowers of his window. "Centrifugal, centripetal," he said, with his chin on his fist. "Stop a planet in its flight, rob it of its centrifugal force, what then? Centripetal has it, and down it falls into the sun! And this —!"

"Do *we* come in the way? I wonder —"

The light of that day went the way of its brethren, and with the later watches of the frosty darkness rose the strange star again. And it was now so bright that the waxing moon seemed but a pale yellow ghost of itself, hanging huge in the sunset. In a South African city a great man had married, and the streets were alight to welcome his return with his bride. "Even the skies have illuminated," said the flatterer. Under Capricorn, two Negro lovers, daring the wild beasts and evil spirits, for love of one another, crouched together in a cane brake where the fire-flies hovered. "That is our star," they whispered, and felt strangely comforted by the sweet brilliance of its light.

The master mathematician sat in his private room and pushed the papers from him. His calculations were already finished. In a small white phial there still remained a little of the drug that had kept him awake and active for four long nights. Each day, serene, explicit, patient as ever, he had given his lecture to his students, and then had come back at once to this momentous calculation. His face was grave, a little drawn and hectic from his drugged activity. For some time he seemed lost in thought. Then he went to the window, and the blind went up with a click. Half way up the sky, over the clustering roofs, chimneys and steeples of the city, hung the star.

He looked at it as one might look into the eyes of a brave enemy. "You may kill me," he said after a silence. "But I can hold you — and all the universe for that matter — in the grip of this little brain. I would not change. Even now."

He looked at the little phial. "There will be no need of sleep again," he said. The next day at noon, punctual to the minute, he entered his lecture theatre, put his hat on the end of the table as his habit was, and carefully selected a large piece of chalk. It was a joke among his students that he could not lecture without that piece of chalk to fumble in his fingers, and once he had been stricken to impotence by their hiding his supply. He came and looked under his grey eyebrows at the rising tiers of young fresh faces, and spoke with his accustomed studied commonness of phrasing. "Circumstances have arisen — circumstances beyond my control," he said and paused, "which will debar me from completing the course I had designed. It would seem, gentlemen, if I may put the thing clearly and briefly, that — Man has lived in vain."

The students glanced at one another. Had they heard aright? Mad? Raised eyebrows and grinning lips there were, but one or two faces remained intent upon his calm grey-fringed face. "It will be interesting," he was saying, "to devote this morning to an exposition, so far as I can make it clear to you, of the calculations that have led me to this conclusion. Let us assume —"

He turned towards the blackboard, meditating a diagram in the way that was usual to him. "What was that about 'lived in vain?' " whispered one student to another. "Listen," said the other, nodding towards the lecturer.

And presently they began to understand.

That night the star rose later, for its proper eastward motion had carried it some way across Leo towards Virgo, and its brightness was so great that the sky became a luminous blue as it rose, and every star was hidden in its turn, save only Jupiter near the zenith, Capella, Aldebaran, Sirius and the pointers of the Bear. It was very white and beautiful. In many parts of the world that night a pallid halo encircled it about. It was perceptibly larger; in the clear refractive sky of the tropics it seemed as if it were nearly a quarter the size of the moon. The frost was still on the ground in England, but the world was as brightly lit as if it were midsummer moonlight. One could see to read quite ordinary print by that cold clear light, and in the cities the lamps burnt yellow and wan.

And everywhere the world was awake that night, and throughout Christendom a sombre murmur hung in the keen air over the countryside like the belling of bees in the heather, and this murmurous tumult grew to a clangour in the cities. It was the tolling of the bells in a million belfry towers and steeples, summoning the people to sleep no more, to sin no more, but to gather in their churches and pray. And overhead, growing larger and brighter, as the earth rolled on its way and the night passed, rose the dazzling star.

And the streets and houses were alight in all the cities, the shipyards glared, and whatever roads led to high country were lit and crowded all night long. And in all the seas about the civilised lands, ships with throbbing engines, and ships with bellying sails, crowded with men and living creatures, were standing out to ocean and the north. For already the warning of the master mathematician had been telegraphed all over the world, and translated into a hundred tongues. The new planet and Neptune, locked in a fiery embrace, were whirling headlong, ever faster and faster towards the sun. Already every second this blazing mass flew a hundred miles, and every second its terrific velocity increased. As it flew now, indeed, it must pass a hundred million of miles wide of the earth and scarcely affect it. But near its destined path, as yet only slightly perturbed, spun the mighty planet Jupiter and his moons sweeping splendid round the sun. Every moment now the attraction between the fiery star and the greatest of the planets grew stronger. And the result of that attraction? Inevitably Jupiter would be deflected from its orbit into an elliptical path, and the burning star, swung by his attraction wide of its sunward rush, would "describe a curved path" and perhaps collide with, and certainly pass very close to, our earth. "Earthquakes, volcanic outbreaks, cyclones, sea waves, floods, and a steady rise in temperature to I know not what limit" — so prophesied the master mathematician.

And overhead, to carry out his words, lonely and cold and livid, blazed the star of the coming doom.

To many who stared at it that night until their eyes ached, it seemed that it was visibly approaching. And that night, too, the weather changed, and the frost that had gripped all Central Europe and France and England softened towards a thaw.

But you must not imagine because I have spoken of people praying through the night and people going aboard ships and people fleeing towards mountainous country that the whole world was already in a terror because of the star. As a matter of fact, use and wont still ruled the world, and save for the talk of idle moments and the splendour of the night, nine human beings out of ten were still busy at their common occupations. In all the cities the shops, save one here and there, opened and closed at their proper hours, the doctor and the undertaker plied their trades, the workers gathered in the factories, soldiers drilled, scholars studied, lovers sought one another, thieves lurked and fled, politicians planned their schemes. The presses of the newspapers roared through the nights, and many a priest of this church and that would not open his holy building to further what he considered a foolish panic. The newspapers insisted on the lesson of the year 1000 — for then, too, people had anticipated the end. The star was no star — mere gas — a comet; and were it a star it could not possibly strike the earth. There was no precedent for such a thing. Common sense was sturdy everywhere, scornful, jesting, a little inclined to persecute the obdurate fearful. That night, at seven-fifteen by Greenwich time, the star would be at its nearest to Jupiter. Then the world would see the turn things would take. The master mathematician's grim warnings were treated by many as so much mere elaborate self-advertisement. Common sense at last, a little heated by argument, signified its unalterable convictions by going to bed. So, too, barbarism and savagery, already tired of the novelty, went about their nightly business, and save for a howling dog here and there, the beast world left the star unheeded.

And yet, when at last the watchers in the European States saw the star rise, an hour later it is true, but no larger than it had been the night before, there were still plenty awake to laugh at the master mathematician — to take the danger as if it had passed.

But hereafter the laughter ceased. The star grew — it grew with a terrible steadiness hour after hour, a little larger each hour, a little nearer the midnight zenith, and brighter and brighter, until it had turned night into a second day. Had it come straight to the earth instead of in a curved path, had it lost no velocity to Jupiter, it must have leapt the intervening gulf in a day, but as it was it took five days altogether to come by our planet. The next night it had become a third the size of the moon before it set to English eyes, and the thaw was assured. It rose over America near the size of the moon, but blinding white to look at, and *hot*; and a breath of hot wind blew now with its rising and gathering strength, and in Virginia, and Brazil, and down the St. Lawrence valley, it shone intermittently through a driving reek of thunderclouds, flickering violet lightning, and hail unprecedented. In Manitoba was a thaw and devastating floods. And upon all the mountains of the earth the snow and ice began to melt that night, and all the rivers coming out of high country flowed thick and turbid, and soon — in their upper reaches — with swirling trees and the bodies of beasts and men. They rose steadily, steadily in the ghostly brilliance, and came trickling over their banks at last, behind the flying population of their valleys.

And along the coast of Argentina and up the South Atlantic the tides were higher than had ever been in the memory of man, and the storms drove the waters in many cases scores of miles inland, drowning whole cities. And so great grew the heat during the night that the rising of the sun was like the coming of a shadow. The earthquakes began and grew until all down America, from the Arctic Circle to Cape Horn, hillsides were sliding, fissures were opening, and houses and walls crumbling to destruction. The whole side of Cotopaxi slipped out in one vast convulsion, and a tumult of lava poured out so high and broad and swift and liquid that in one day it reached the sea.

So the star, with the wan moon in its wake, marched across the Pacific, trailed the thunderstorms like the hem of a robe, and the growing tidal wave that toiled behind it, frothing and eager, poured over island and island and swept them clear of men. Until that wave came at last — in a blinding light and with the breath of a furnace, swift and terrible it came — a wall of water, fifty feet high, roaring hungrily, upon the long coasts of Asia, and swept inland across the plains of China. For a space the star, hotter now and larger and brighter than the sun in its strength, showed with pitiless brilliance the wide and populous country; towns and villages with their pagodas and trees, roads, wide cultivated fields, millions of sleepless people staring in helpless terror at the incandescent sky; and then, low and growing, came the murmur of the flood. And thus it was with millions of men that night — a flight nowhither, with limbs heavy with heat and breath fierce and scant, and the flood like a wall swift and white behind. And then death.

China was lit glowing white, but over Japan and Java and all the islands of Eastern Asia the great star was a ball of dull red fire because of the steam and smoke and ashes the volcanoes were spouting forth to salute its coming. Above was the lava, hot gases and ash, and below the seething floods, and the whole earth swayed and rumbled with the earthquake shocks. Soon the immemorial snows of Tibet and the Himalaya were melting and pouring down by ten million deepening converging channels upon the plains of Burmah and Hindostan. The tangled summits of the Indian jungles were aflame in a thousand places, and below the hurrying waters around the stems were dark objects that still struggled feebly and reflected the blood-red tongues of fire. And in a rudderless confusion a multitude of men and women fled down the broad river-ways to that one last hope of men — the open sea.

Larger grew the star, and larger, hotter, and brighter with a terrible swiftness now. The tropical ocean had lost its phosphorescence, and the whirling steam rose in ghostly wreaths from the black waves that plunged incessantly, speckled with storm-tossed ships.

And then came a wonder. It seemed to those who in Europe watched for the rising of the star that the world must have ceased its rotation. In a thousand open spaces of down and upland the people who had fled thither from the floods and the falling houses and sliding slopes of hill watched for that rising in vain. Hour followed hour through a terrible suspense, and the star rose not. Once again men set their eyes upon the old constellations they had counted lost to them forever. In England it was hot and clear overhead, though the ground quivered perpetually, but in the tropics, Sirius and

Capella and Aldebaran showed through a veil of steam. And when at last the great star rose near ten hours late, the sun rose close upon it, and in the centre of its white heart was a disc of black.

Over Asia it was the star had begun to fall behind the movement of the sky, and then suddenly, as it hung over India, its light had been veiled. All the plain of India from the mouth of the Indus to the mouths of the Ganges was a shallow waste of shining water that night, out of which rose temples and palaces, mounds and hills, black with people. Every minaret was a clustering mass of people, who fell one by one into the turbid waters, as heat and terror overcame them. The whole land seemed a-wailing, and suddenly there swept a shadow across that furnace of despair, and a breath of cold wind, and a gathering of clouds, out of the cooling air. Men looking up, near blinded, at the star, saw that a black disc was creeping across the light. It was the moon, coming between the star and the earth. And even as men cried to God at this respite, out of the East with a strange inexplicable swiftness sprang the sun. And then star, sun and moon rushed together across the heavens.

So it was that presently, to the European watchers, star and sun rose close upon each other, drove headlong for a space and then slower, and at last came to rest, star and sun merged into one glare of flame at the zenith of the sky. The moon no longer eclipsed the star but was lost to sight in the brilliance of the sky. And though those who were still alive regarded it for the most part with that dull stupidity that hunger, fatigue, heat and despair engender, there were still men who could perceive the meaning of these signs. Star and earth had been at their nearest, had swung about one another, and the star had passed. Already it was receding, swifter and swifter, in the last stage of its headlong journey downward into the sun.

And then the clouds gathered, blotting out the vision of the sky, the thunder and lightning wove a garment round the world; all over the earth was such a downpour of rain as men had never before seen, and where the volcanoes flared red against the cloud canopy there descended torrents of mud. Everywhere the waters were pouring off the land, leaving mud-silted ruins, and the earth littered like a storm-worn beach with all that had floated, and the dead bodies of the men and brutes, its children. For days the water streamed off the land, sweeping away soil and trees and houses in the way, and piling huge dykes and scooping out Titanic gullies over the country-side. Those were the days of darkness that followed the star and the heat. All through them, and for many weeks and months, the earthquakes continued.

But the star had passed, and men, hunger-driven and gathering courage only slowly, might creep back to their ruined cities, buried granaries, and sodden fields. Such few ships as had escaped the storms of that time came stunned and shattered and sounding their way cautiously through the new marks and shoals of once familiar ports. And as the storms subsided men perceived that everywhere the days were hotter than of yore, and the sun larger, and the moon, shrunk to a third of its former size, took now fourscore days between its new and new.

But of the new brotherhood that grew presently among men, of the saving of laws and books and machines, of the strange change that had come over Iceland and Greenland and the shores of Baffin's Bay, so that the sailors coming there presently found them green and gracious, and could scarce believe their eyes, this story does not tell. Nor of the movement of mankind now that the earth was hotter, northward and southward towards the poles of the earth. It concerns itself only with the coming and the passing of the Star.

The Martian astronomers — for there are astronomers on Mars, although they are very different beings from men — were naturally profoundly interested by these things. They saw them from their own standpoint of course. "Considering the mass and temperature of the missile that was flung through our solar system into the sun," one wrote, "it is astonishing what a little damage the earth, which it missed so narrowly, has sustained. All the familiar continental markings and the masses of the seas remain intact, and indeed the only difference seems to be a shrinkage of the white discoloration (supposed to be frozen water) round either pole." Which only shows how small the vastest of human catastrophes may seem, at a distance of a few million miles.

THE NEW ACCELERATOR

I can still remember the excitement of first reading this story when I was twelve. As a charter subscriber to Hugo Gernsback's *Amazing Stories,* I read "The New Accelerator" when it was reprinted in the first issue (April 1926) of the first magazine devoted exclusively to science fiction. Would that I had preserved those early issues! They would be worth a lot of money to collectors today.

That one could increase the velocity of electrical impulses through the nervous system and the brain may not be too outlandish a notion, but a heart beating a thousand times faster presents serious difficulties. Blood pressure would burst arteries, not to mention the heat produced by the friction of fast-flowing blood. Vocal cords would be vibrating a thousand times faster, raising the frequency of sound waves far too high for the ear to hear. Moreover, sound would still travel at the same rate through air, making it impossible for two men to have long conversations in just a few microseconds.

Of course Wells, a trained biologist, would have been aware of such problems, but facts often have to be neglected in science fiction for the sake of a good yarn. Wells himself once described his science fiction as "impossible" in contrast to the work of Jules Verne.

"The New Accelerator" first ran in *The Strand* (December 1901). This was before moving pictures accustomed audiences to slow- and fast-motion effects produced by running the camera faster or slower than usual. It was also four years before Einstein's first paper on special relativity made clear that time was relative.

In Einstein's famous clock paradox, a person could travel long distances at high speed, and only a few weeks would go by on the spaceship while years flashed by on earth. Similarly, the accelerator drug allows the narrator to write his entire story in one sitting while six minutes pass in the outside world. I suspect that my boyhood wonder at Wells's demonstration of time's relativity had an influence on my later efforts to understand the essentials of relativity theory.

❧

CERTAINLY, if ever a man found a guinea when he was looking for a pin it is my good friend Professor Gibberne. I have heard before of investigators overshooting the mark, but never quite to the extent that he has done.

He has really, this time at any rate, without any touch of exaggeration in the phrase, found something to revolutionise human life. And that when he was simply seeking an all-round nervous stimulant to bring languid people up to the stresses of these pushful days. I have tasted the stuff now several times, and I cannot do better than describe the effect the thing had on me. That there are astonishing experiences in store for all in search of new sensations will become apparent enough.

Professor Gibberne, as many people know, is my neighbour in Folkestone. Unless my memory plays me a trick, his portrait at various ages has already appeared in *The Strand Magazine* — I think late in 1899; but I am unable to look it up because I have lent that volume to some one who has never sent it back. The reader may, perhaps, recall the high forehead and the singularly long black eyebrows that give such a Mephistophelian touch to his face. He occupies one of those pleasant little detached houses in the mixed style that make the western end of the Upper Sandgate Road so interesting. His is the one with the Flemish gables and the Moorish portico, and it is in the little room with the mullioned bay window that he works when he is down here, and in which of an evening we have so often smoked and talked together. He is a mighty jester, but, besides, he likes to talk to me about his work; he is one of those men who find a help and stimulus in talking, and so I have been able to follow the conception of the New Accelerator right up from a very early stage. Of course, the greater portion of his experimental work is not done in Folkestone, but in Gower Street, in the fine new laboratory next to the hospital that he has been the first to use.

As every one knows, or at least as all intelligent people know, the special department in which Gibberne has gained so great and deserved a reputation among physiologists is the action of drugs upon the nervous system. Upon soporifics, sedatives, and anæsthetics he is, I am told, unequalled. He is also a chemist of considerable eminence, and I suppose in the subtle and complex jungle of riddles that centres about the ganglion cell and the axis fibre there are little cleared places of his making, little glades of illumination, that, until he sees fit to publish his results, are still inaccessible to every other living man. And in the last few years he has been particularly assiduous upon this question of nervous stimulants, and already, before the discovery of the New Accelerator, very successful with them. Medical science has to thank him for at least three distinct and absolutely safe invigorators of unrivalled value to practising men. In cases of exhaustion the preparation known as Gibberne's B Syrup has, I suppose, saved more lives already than any lifeboat round the coast.

"But none of these little things begin to satisfy me yet," he told me nearly a year ago. "Either they increase the central energy without affecting the nerves or they simply increase the available energy by lowering the nervous conductivity; and all of them are unequal and local in their operation. One wakes up the heart and viscera and leaves the brain stupefied, one gets at the brain champagne fashion and does nothing good for the solar plexus, and what I want — and what, if it's an earthly possibility, I mean to have — is a stimulant that stimulates all round, that wakes you up for a time from the crown of your head to the tip of your great toe, and makes you go two — or even three to everybody else's one. Eh? That's the thing I'm after."

"It would tire a man," I said.

"Not a doubt of it. And you'd eat double or treble — and all that. But just think what the thing would mean. Imagine yourself with a little phial like this" — he held up a little bottle of green glass and marked his points with it — "and in this precious phial is the power to think twice as fast, move twice as quickly, do twice as much work in a given time as you could otherwise do."

"But is such a thing possible?"

"I believe so. If it isn't, I've wasted my time for a year. These various preparations of the hypophosphites, for example, seem to show that something of the sort . . . Even if it was only one and a half times as fast it would do."

"It *would* do," I said.

"If you were a statesman in a corner, for example, time rushing up against you, something urgent to be done, eh?"

"He could dose his private secretary," I said.

"And gain — double time. And think if *you*, for example, wanted to finish a book."

"Usually," I said, "I wish I'd never begun 'em."

"Or a doctor, driven to death, wants to sit down and think out a case. Or a barrister — or a man cramming for an examination."

"Worth a guinea a drop," said I, "and more — to men like that."

"And in a duel, again," said Gibberne, "where it all depends on your quickness in pulling the trigger."

"Or in fencing," I echoed.

"You see," said Gibberne, "if I get it as an all-round thing it will really do you no harm at all — except perhaps to an infinitesimal degree it brings you nearer old age. You will just have lived twice to other people's once ——"

"I suppose," I meditated, "in a duel — it would be fair?"

"That's a question for the seconds," said Gibberne.

I harked back further. "And you really think such a thing *is* possible?" I said.

"As possible," said Gibberne, and glanced at something that went throbbing by the window, "as a motor-bus. As a matter of fact ——"

He paused and smiled at me deeply, and tapped slowly on the edge of his desk with the green phial. "I think I know the stuff. . . . Already I've got something coming." The nervous smile upon his face betrayed the gravity of his revelation. He rarely talked of his actual experimental work unless things were very near the end. "And it may be, it may be — I shouldn't be surprised — it may even do the thing at a greater rate than twice."

"It will be rather a big thing," I hazarded.

"It will be, I think, rather a big thing."

But I don't think he quite knew what a big thing it was to be, for all that.

I remember we had several talks about the stuff after that. "The New Accelerator" he called it, and his tone about it grew more confident on each occasion. Sometimes he talked nervously of unexpected physiological results its use might have, and then he would get a little unhappy; at others he was frankly mercenary, and we debated long and anxiously how the preparation might be turned to commercial account. "It's a good thing," said Gibberne, "a tremendous thing. I know I'm giving the world something, and I think it only reasonable we should expect the world to pay. The dignity of science is all very well, but I think somehow I must have the monopoly of the stuff for, say, ten years. I don't see why *all* the fun in life should go to the dealers in ham."

My own interest in the coming drug certainly did not wane in the time. I have always had a queer little twist towards metaphysics in my mind. I have always been given to paradoxes about space and time, and it seemed to me that Gibberne was really preparing no less than the absolute acceleration of life. Suppose a man repeatedly dosed with such a preparation: he would live an active and record life indeed, but he would be an adult at eleven, middle-aged at twenty-five, and by thirty well on the road to senile decay. It seemed to me that so far Gibberne was only going to do for any one who took his drug exactly what Nature has done for the Jews and Orientals, who are men in their teens and aged by fifty, and quicker in thought and act than we are all the time. The marvel of drugs has always been great to my mind; you can madden a man, calm a man, make him incredibly strong and alert or a helpless log, quicken this passion and allay that, all by means of drugs, and here was a new miracle to be added to this strange armoury of phials the doctors use! But Gibberne was far too eager upon his technical points to enter very keenly into my aspect of the question.

It was the 7th or 8th of August when he told me the distillation that would decide his failure or success for a time was going forward as we talked, and it was on the 10th that he told me the thing was done and the New Accelerator a tangible reality in the world. I met him as I was going up the Sandgate Hill towards Folkestone — I think I was going to get my hair cut, and he came hurrying down to meet me — I suppose he was coming to my house to tell me at once of his success. I remember that his eyes were unusually bright and his face flushed, and I noted even the swift alacrity of his step.

"It's done," he cried, and gripped my hand, speaking very fast; "it's more than done. Come up to my house and see."

"Really?"

"Really!" he shouted. "Incredibly! Come up and see."

"And it does — twice?"

"It does more, much more. It scares me. Come up and see the stuff. Taste it! Try it! It's the most amazing stuff on earth." He gripped my arm and, walking at such a pace that he forced me into a trot, went shouting with me up the hill. A whole *char-à-banc*-ful of people turned and stared at us in unison after the manner of people in *chars-à-banc*. It was one of those hot, clear days that Folkestone sees so much of, every colour incredibly bright and every outline hard. There was a breeze, of course, but not so much breeze as sufficed under these conditions to keep me cool and dry. I panted for mercy.

"I'm not walking fast, am I?" cried Gibberne, and slackened his pace to a quick march.

"You've been taking some of this stuff," I puffed.

"No," he said. "At the utmost a drop of water that stood in a beaker from which I had washed out the last traces of the stuff. I took some last night, you know. But that is ancient history, now."

"And it goes twice?" I said, nearing his doorway in a grateful perspiration.

"It goes a thousand times, many thousand times!" cried Gibberne, with a dramatic gesture, flinging open his Early English carved oak gate.

"Phew!" said I, and followed him to the door.

"I don't know how many times it goes," he said, with his latch-key in his hand.

"And you ——"

"It throws all sorts of light on nervous physiology, it kicks the theory of vision into a perfectly new shape! . . . Heaven knows how many thousand times. We'll try all that after —— The thing is to try the stuff now."

"Try the stuff?" I said, as we went along the passage.

"Rather," said Gibberne, turning on me in his study. "There it is in that little green phial there! Unless you happen to be afraid?"

I am a careful man by nature, and only theoretically adventurous. I *was* afraid. But on the other hand there is pride.

"Well," I haggled. "You say you've tried it?"

"I've tried it," he said, "and I don't look hurt by it, do I? I don't even look livery and I *feel* ——"

I sat down. "Give me the potion," I said. "If the worst comes to the worst it will save having my hair cut, and that I think is one of the most hateful duties of a civilised man. How do you take the mixture?"

"With water," said Gibberne, whacking down a carafe.

He stood up in front of his desk and regarded me in his easy chair; his manner was suddenly affected by a touch of the Harley Street specialist. "It's rum stuff, you know," he said.

I made a gesture with my hand.

"I must warn you in the first place as soon as you've got it down to shut your eyes, and open them very cautiously in a minute or so's time. One still sees. The sense of vision is a question of length of vibration, and not of multitude of impacts; but there's a kind of shock to the retina, a nasty giddy confusion just at the time, if the eyes are open. Keep 'em shut."

"Shut," I said. "Good!"

"And the next thing is, keep still. Don't begin to whack about. You may fetch something a nasty rap if you do. Remember you will be going several thousand times faster than you ever did before, heart, lungs, muscles, brain — everything — and you will hit hard without knowing it. You won't know it, you know. You'll feel just as you do now. Only everything in the world will seem to be going ever so many thousand times slower that it ever went before. That's what makes it so deuced queer."

"Lor'," I said. "And you mean ———"

"You'll see," said he, and took up a little measure. He glanced at the material on his desk. "Glasses," he said, "water. All here. Mustn't take too much for the first attempt."

The little phial glucked out its precious contents. "Don't forget what I told you," he said, turning the contents of the measure into a glass in the manner of an Italian waiter measuring whisky. "Sit with the eyes tightly shut and in absolute stillness for two minutes," he said. "Then you will hear me speak."

He added an inch or so of water to the little dose in each glass.

"By-the-by," he said, "don't put your glass down. Keep it in your hand and rest your hand on your knee. Yes — so. And now ———"

He raised his glass.

"The New Accelerator," I said.

"The New Accelerator," he answered, and we touched glasses and drank, and instantly I closed my eyes.

You know that blank non-existence into which one drops when one has taken "gas." For an indefinite interval it was like that. Then I heard Gibberne telling me to wake up, and I stirred and opened my eyes. There he stood as he had been standing, glass still in hand. It was empty, that was all the difference.

"Well?" said I.

"Nothing out of the way?"

"Nothing. A slight feeling of exhilaration, perhaps. Nothing more."

"Sounds?"

"Things are still," I said. "By Jove! yes! They *are* still. Except the sort of faint pat, patter, like rain falling on different things. What is it?"

"Analysed sounds," I think he said, but I am not sure. He glanced at the window. "Have you ever seen a curtain before a window fixed in that way before?"

I followed his eyes, and there was the end of the curtain, frozen, as it were, corner high, in the act of flapping briskly in the breeze.

"No," said I; "that's odd."

"And here," he said, and opened the hand that held the glass. Naturally I winced, expecting the glass to smash. But so far from smashing it did not even seem to stir; it hung in mid-air — motionless. "Roughly speaking," said Gibberne, "an object in these latitudes falls 16 feet in the first second. This glass is falling 16 feet in a second now. Only, you see, it hasn't been falling yet for the hundredth part of a second. That gives you some idea of the pace of my Accelerator." And he waved his hand round and round, over and under the slowly sinking glass. Finally he took it by the bottom, pulled it down, and placed it very carefully on the table. "Eh?" he said to me, and laughed.

"That seems all right," I said, and began very gingerly to raise myself from my chair. I felt perfectly well, very light and comfortable, and quite confident in my mind. I was going fast all over. My heart, for example, was beating a thousand times a second, but that caused me no discomfort at all. I looked out of the window. An immovable cyclist, head down and with a frozen puff of dust behind his driving-wheel, scorched to overtake a galloping *char-à-banc* that did not stir. I gaped in amazement at this incredible spectacle. "Gibberne," I cried, "how long will this confounded stuff last?"

"Heaven knows!" he answered. "Last time I took it I went to bed and slept it off. I tell you, I was frightened. It must have lasted some minutes, I think — it seemed like hours. But after a bit it slows down rather suddenly, I believe."

I was proud to observe that I did not feel frightened — I suppose because there were two of us. "Why shouldn't we go out?" I asked.

"Why not?"

"They'll see us."

"Not they. Goodness, no! Why, we shall be going a thousand times faster than the quickest conjuring trick that was ever done. Come along! Which way shall we go? Window, or door?"

And out by the window we went.

Assuredly of all the strange experiences that I have ever had, or imagined, or read of other people having or imagining, that little raid I made with Gibberne on the Folkestone Leas, under the influence of the New Accelerator, was the strangest and maddest of all. We went out by his gate into the road, and there we made a minute examination of the statuesque passing traffic. The tops of the wheels and some of the legs of the horses of this *char-à-banc*, the end of the whip-lash and the lower jaw of the conductor — who was just beginning to yawn — were perceptibly in motion, but all the rest of the lumbering conveyance seemed still. And quite noiseless except for a faint rattling that came from one man's throat! And as parts of this frozen edifice there were a driver, you know, and a conductor, and eleven people! The effect as we walked about the thing began by being madly queer, and ended by being — disagreeable. There they were, people like ourselves and yet not like ourselves, frozen in careless attitudes, caught in mid-gesture. A girl and a man smiled at one another, a leering smile that threatened to last for evermore; a woman in a floppy capelline rested her arm on the rail and stared at Gibberne's house with the unwinking stare of eternity; a man stroked his moustache like a figure of wax, and another stretched a tiresome stiff hand with extended fingers towards his loosened hat. We stared at them, we laughed at them, we made faces at them, and then a sort of disgust of them came upon us, and we turned away and walked round in front of the cyclist towards the Leas.

"Goodness!" cried Gibberne, suddenly; "look there!"

He pointed, and there at the tip of his finger and sliding down the air with wings flapping slowly and at the speed of an exceptionally languid snail — was a bee.

And so we came out upon the Leas. There the thing seemed madder than ever. The band was playing in the upper stand, though all the sound it made for us was a low-pitched, wheezy rattle, a sort of prolonged last sigh that passed at times into a sound like the slow, muffled ticking of some monstrous clock. Frozen people stood erect, strange, silent, self-conscious-looking dummies hung unstably in mid-stride, promenading upon the grass. I passed close to a little poodle dog suspended in the act of leaping, and watched the slow movement of his legs as he sank to the earth. "Lord, look *here!*" cried Gibberne, and we halted for a moment before a magnificent person in white faint-striped flannels, white shoes, and a Panama hat, who turned back to wink at two gaily dressed ladies he had passed. A wink, studied with such leisurely deliberation as we could afford, is an unattractive thing.

It loses any quality of alert gaiety, and one remarks that the winking eye does not completely close, that under its drooping lid appears the lower edge of an eyeball and a little line of white. "Heaven give me memory," said I, "and I will never wink again."

"Or smile," said Gibberne, with his eye on the lady's answering teeth.

"It's infernally hot, somehow," said I. "Let's go slower."

"Oh, come along!" said Gibberne.

We picked our way among the bath-chairs in the path. Many of the people sitting in the chairs seemed almost natural in their passive poses, but the contorted scarlet of the bandsmen was not a restful thing to see. A purple-faced little gentleman was frozen in the midst of a violent struggle to refold his newspaper against the wind; there were many evidences that all these people in their sluggish way were exposed to a considerable breeze, a breeze that had no existence so far as our sensations went. We came out and walked a little way from the crowd, and turned and regarded it. To see all that multitude changed to a picture, smitten rigid, as it were, into the semblance of realistic wax, was impossibly wonderful. It was absurd, of course; but it filled me with an irrational, an exultant sense of superior advantage. Consider the wonder of it! All that I had said, and thought, and done since the stuff had begun to work in my veins had happened, so far as those people, so far as the world in general went, in the twinkling of an eye. "The New Accelerator ——" I began, but Gibberne interrupted me.

"There's that infernal old woman!" he said.

"What old woman?"

"Lives next door to me," said Gibberne. "Has a lapdog that yaps. Gods! The temptation is strong!"

There is something very boyish and impulsive about Gibberne at times. Before I could expostulate with him he had dashed forward, snatched the unfortunate animal out of visible existence, and was running violently with it towards the cliff of the Leas. It was most extraordinary. The little brute, you know, didn't bark or wriggle or make the slightest sign of vitality. It kept quite stiffly in an attitude of somnolent repose, and Gibberne held it by the neck. It was like running about with a dog of wood. "Gibberne," I cried, "put it down!" Then I said something else. "If you run like that, Gibberne," I cried, "you'll set your clothes on fire. Your linen trousers are going brown as it is!"

He clapped his hand on his thigh and stood hesitating on the verge. "Gibberne," I cried, coming up, "put it down. This heat is too much! It's our running so! Two or three miles a second! Friction of the air!"

"What?" he said, glancing at the dog.

"Friction of the air," I shouted. "Friction of the air. Going too fast. Like meteorites and things. Too hot. And, Gibberne! Gibberne! I'm all over pricking and a sort of perspiration. You can see people stirring slightly. I believe the stuff's working off! Put that dog down."

"Eh?" he said.

"It's working off," I repeated. "We're too hot and the stuff's working off! I'm wet through."

He stared at me. Then at the band, the wheezy rattle of whose performance was certainly going faster. Then with a tremendous sweep of the arm he hurled the dog away from him and it went spinning upward, still inanimate, and hung at last over the grouped parasols of a knot of chattering people. Gibberne was gripping my elbow. "By Jove!" he cried. "I believe it is! A sort of hot pricking and — yes. That man's moving his pocket-handkerchief! Perceptibly. We must get out of this sharp."

But we could not get out of it sharply enough. Luckily, perhaps! For we might have run, and if we had run we should, I believe, have burst into flames. Almost certainly we should have burst into flames! You know we had neither of us thought of that. . . . But before we could even begin to run the action of the drug had ceased. It was the business of a minute fraction of a second. The effect of the New Accelerator passed like the drawing of a curtain, vanished in the movement of a hand. I heard Gibberne's voice in infinite alarm. "Sit down," he said, and flop, down upon the turf at the edge of the Leas I sat — scorching as I sat. There is a patch of burnt grass there still where I sat down. The whole stagnation seemed to wake up as I did so, the disarticulated vibration of the band rushed together into a blast of music, the promenaders put their feet down and walked their ways, the papers and flags began flapping, smiles passed into words, the winker finished his wink and went on his way complacently, and all the seated people moved and spoke.

The whole world had come alive again, was going as fast as we were, or rather we were going no faster than the rest of the world. It was like slowing down as one comes into a railway station. Everything seemed to spin round for a second or two, I had the most transient feeling of nausea, and that was all. And the little dog which had seemed to hang for a moment when the force of Gibberne's arm was expended fell with a swift acceleration clean through a lady's parasol!

That was the saving of us. Unless it was for one corpulent old gentleman in a bath-chair, who certainly did start at the sight of us and afterwards regarded us at intervals with a darkly suspicious eye, and, finally, I believe, said something to his nurse about us, I doubt if a solitary person remarked our sudden appearance among them. Plop! We must have appeared abruptly. We ceased to smoulder almost at once, though the turf beneath me was uncomfortably hot. The attention of every one — including even the Amusements' Association band, which on this occasion, for the only time in its history, got out of tune — was arrested by the amazing fact, and the still more amazing yapping and uproar caused by the fact that a respectable, over-fed lap-dog sleeping quietly to the east of the bandstand should suddenly fall through the parasol of a lady on the west — in a slightly singed condition due to the extreme velocity of its movements through the air. In these absurd days, too, when we are all trying to be as psychic, and silly, and superstitious as possible! People got up and trod on other people, chairs were overturned, the Leas policeman ran. How the matter settled itself I do not know — we were much too anxious to disentangle ourselves from the affair and get out of range of the eye of the old gentleman in the bath-chair to make minute inquiries. As soon as we were sufficiently cool and sufficiently recovered from our giddiness and nausea and confusion of mind to do so we stood up and, skirting the crowd, directed our steps back along the road below the Metropole towards Gibberne's house. But amidst the din I heard very distinctly the gentleman who had been sitting beside the lady of the ruptured sunshade using quite unjustifiable threats and language to one of those chair-attendants who have "Inspector" written on their caps. "If you didn't throw the dog," he said, "who *did?*"

The sudden return of movement and familiar noises, and our natural anxiety about ourselves (our clothes were still dreadfully hot, and the fronts of the thighs of Gibberne's white trousers were scorched a drabbish brown), prevented the minute observations I should have liked to make on all these things. Indeed, I really made no observations of any scientific value on that return. The bee, of course, had gone. I looked for that cyclist, but he was already out of sight as we came into the Upper Sandgate Road or hidden from us by traffic; the *char-à-banc,* however, with its people now all alive and stirring, was clattering along at a spanking pace almost abreast of the nearer church.

We noted, however, that the window-sill on which we had stepped in getting out of the house was slightly singed, and that the impressions of our feet on the gravel of the path were unusually deep.

So it was I had my first experience of the New Accelerator. Practically we had been running about and saying and doing all sorts of things in the space of a second or so of time. We had lived half an hour while the band had played, perhaps, two bars. But the effect it had upon us was that the whole world had stopped for our convenient inspection. Considering all things, and particularly considering our rashness in venturing out of the house, the experience might certainly have been much more disagreeable than it was. It showed, no doubt, that Gibberne has still much to learn before his preparation is a manageable convenience, but its practicability it certainly demonstrated beyond all cavil.

Since that adventure he has been steadily bringing its use under control, and I have several times, and without the slightest bad result, taken measured doses under his direction; though I must confess I have not yet ventured abroad again while under its influence. I may mention, for example, that this story has been written at one sitting and without interruption, except for the nibbling of some chocolate, by its means. I began at 6:25, and my watch is now very nearly at the minute past the half-hour. The convenience of securing a long, uninterrupted spell of work in the midst of a day full of engagements cannot be exaggerated. Gibberne is now working at the quantitative handling of his preparation, with especial reference to its distinctive effects upon different types of constitution. He then hopes to find a Retarder with which to dilute its present rather excessive potency. The Retarder will, of course, have the reverse effect to the Accelerator; used alone it should enable the patient to spread a few seconds over many hours of ordinary time, and so to maintain an apathetic inaction, a glacier-like absence of alacrity, amidst the most animated or irritating surroundings. The two things together must necessarily work an entire revolution in civilised existence. It is the beginning of our escape from that Time Garment of which Carlyle speaks. While this Accelerator will enable us to concentrate ourselves with tremendous impact upon any moment or occasion that demands our utmost sense and vigour, the Retarder will enable us to pass in passive tranquillity through infinite hardship and tedium. Perhaps I am a little optimistic about the Retarder, which has indeed still to be discovered, but about the Accelerator there is no possible sort of doubt whatever. Its appearance upon the market in a convenient, controllable, and assimilable form is a matter of the next few months. It will be obtainable of all chemists and druggists, in small green bottles, at a high but, considering its extraordinary qualities, by no means excessive price. Gibberne's Nervous Accelerator it will be called, and he hopes to be able to supply it in three strengths: one in 200, one in 900, and one in 2000, distinguished by yellow, pink, and white labels respectively.

No doubt its use renders a great number of very extraordinary things possible; for, of course, the most remarkable and, possibly, even criminal proceedings may be effected with impunity by thus dodging, as it were, into the interstices of time. Like all potent preparations it will be liable to abuse. We have, however, discussed this aspect of the question very thoroughly, and we have decided that this is purely a matter of medical jurisprudence and altogether outside our province. We shall manufacture and sell the Accelerator, and, as for the consequences — we shall see.

THE REMARKABLE CASE OF DAVIDSON'S EYES

In my opinion, the evidence for remote viewing, or what used to be called clairvoyance, is close to zero. It certainly is true that parapsychologists have not the foggiest idea of how it could work, especially in view of their belief that it is independent of both time and distance. The explanation put forth in this early story by Wells is as good as any.

Davidson's head is between the poles of a powerful electromagnet when a lightning bolt strikes the laboratory. As a result his eyes become attached to a "kink," or what later science fiction calls a "warp," in space-time. For three weeks Davidson's eyes seem to be located on an island eight thousand miles away.

Just as two widely separated points in Flatland can be brought together by folding the plane, Wells explains, so two widely separated points in space can be brought together by folding space through a fourth dimension. Today's far-out cosmologists speak seriously of "wormholes" joining parts of space by way of a higher dimension. In superstring theory, for the first time in the history of physics, higher space dimensions are considered by many physicists to be as real as three-dimensional space.

Wells was fascinated by the concept of higher dimensions. In "The Plattner Story" an explosion propels a man into the fourth dimension. When another explosion sends him back he is left–right reversed, like lifting a resident of Flatland off the plane, turning him over and putting him down again. Wells's great Utopia novel *Men like Gods* made an early use of parallel universes lying side by side in the fourth dimension like the pages of a book.

"The Remarkable Case of Davidson's Eyes" was first published in *The Pall Mall Budget* (March 28, 1895).

I

THE transitory mental aberration of Sidney Davidson, remarkable enough in itself, is still more remarkable if Wade's explanation is to be credited. It sets one dreaming of the oddest possibilities of intercommunication in the future, of spending an intercalary five minutes on the other side of the world, or being watched in our most secret operations by unsuspected eyes. It happened that I was the immediate witness of Davidson's seizure, and so it falls naturally to me to put the story upon paper.

When I say that I was the immediate witness of his seizure, I mean that I was the first on the scene. The thing happened at the Harlow Technical College just beyond the Highgate Archway. He was alone in the larger laboratory when the thing happened. I was in the smaller room, where the balances are, writing up some notes. The thunderstorm had completely upset my work, of course. It was just after one of the louder peals that I thought I heard some glass smash in the other room. I stopped writing, and turned round to listen. For a moment I heard nothing; the hail was playing the devil's tattoo on the corrugated zinc of the roof. Then came another sound, a smash — no doubt of it this time. Something heavy had been knocked off the bench. I jumped up at once and went and opened the door leading into the big laboratory.

I was surprised to hear a queer sort of laugh, and saw Davidson standing unsteadily in the middle of the room, with a dazzled look on his face. My first impression was that he was drunk. He did not notice me. He was clawing out at something invisible a yard in front of his face. He put out his hand, slowly, rather hesitatingly, and then clutched nothing. "What's come to it?" he said. He held up his hands to his face, fingers spread out. "Great Scott!" he said. The thing happened three or four years ago, when every one swore by that personage. Then he began raising his feet clumsily, as though he had expected to find them glued to the floor.

"Davidson!" cried I. "What's the matter with you?" He turned round in my direction and looked about for me. He looked over me and at me and on either side of me, without the slightest sign of seeing me. "Waves," he said; "and a remarkably neat schooner. I'd swear that was Bellows's voice. *Hullo!*" He shouted suddenly at the top of his voice.

I thought he was up to some foolery. Then I saw littered about his feet the shattered remains of the best of our electrometers. "What's up, man?" said I. "You've smashed the electrometer!"

"Bellows again!" said he. "Friends left, if my hands are gone. Something about electrometers. Which way *are* you, Bellows?" He suddenly came staggering towards me. "The damned stuff cuts like butter," he said. He walked straight into the bench and recoiled. "None so buttery, that!" he said, and stood swaying.

I felt scared. "Davidson," said I, "what on earth's come over you?"

He looked round him in every direction. "I could swear that was Bellows. Why don't you show yourself like a man, Bellows?"

It occurred to me that he must be suddenly struck blind. I walked round the table and laid my hand upon his arm. I never saw a man more startled in my life. He jumped away from me, and came round into an attitude of self-defence, his face fairly distorted with terror. "Good God!" he cried. "What was that?"

"It's I — Bellows. Confound it, Davidson!"

He jumped when I answered him and stared — how can I express it? — right through me. He began talking, not to me, but to himself. "Here in broad daylight on a clear beach. Not a place to hide in." He looked about him wildly. "Here! I'm *off*." He suddenly turned and ran headlong into the big electro-magnet — so violently that, as we found afterwards, he bruised his shoulder and jawbone cruelly. At that he stepped back a pace, and cried out with almost a whimper, "What, in Heaven's name, has come over me?" He stood, blanched with terror and trembling violently, with his right arm clutching his left, where that had collided with the magnet.

By that time I was excited, and fairly excited. "Davidson," said I, "don't be afraid."

He was startled at my voice, but not so excessively as before. I repeated my words in as clear and firm a tone as I could assume. "Bellows," he said, "is that you?"

"Can't you see it's me?"

He laughed. "I can't even see it's myself. Where the devil are we?"

"Here," said I, "in the laboratory."

"The laboratory!" he answered, in a puzzled tone, and put his hand to his forehead. "I *was* in the laboratory — till that flash came, but I'm hanged if I'm there now. What ship is that?"

"There's no ship," said I. "Do be sensible, old chap."

"No ship!" he repeated, and seemed to forget my denial forthwith. "I suppose," said he, slowly, "we're both dead. But the rummy part is I feel just as though I still had a body. Don't get used to it all at once, I suppose. The old shop was struck by lightning, I suppose. Jolly quick thing, Bellows — eigh?"

"Don't talk nonsense. You're very much alive. You are in the laboratory, blundering about. You've just smashed a new electrometer. I don't envy you when Boyce arrives."

He stared away from me towards the diagrams of cryohydrates. "I must be deaf," said he. "They've fired a gun, for there goes the puff of smoke, and I never heard a sound."

I put my hand on his arm again, and this time he was less alarmed. "We seem to have a sort of invisible bodies," said he. "By Jove! there's a boat coming round the headland! It's very much like the old life after all — in a different climate."

I shook his arm. "Davidson," I cried, "wake up!"

II

It was just then that Boyce came in. So soon as he spoke Davidson exclaimed: "Old Boyce! Dead too! What a lark!" I hastened to explain that Davidson was in a kind of somnambulistic trance. Boyce was interested at once. We both did all we could to rouse the fellow out of his extraordinary state. He answered our questions, and asked us some of his own, but his attention seemed distracted by his hallucination about a beach and a ship. He kept interpolating observations concerning some boat and the davits and sails filling with the wind. It made one feel queer, in the dusky laboratory, to hear him saying such things.

He was blind and helpless. We had to walk him down the passage, one at each elbow, to Boyce's private room, and while Boyce talked to him there, and humoured him about this ship idea, I went along the corridor and asked old Wade to come and look at him. The voice of our Dean sobered him a little, but not very much. He asked where his hands were, and why he had to walk about up to his waist in the ground. Wade thought over him a long time — you know how he knits his brows — and then made him feel the couch, guiding his hands to it. "That's a couch," said Wade. "The couch in the private room of Professor Boyce. Horsehair stuffing."

Davidson felt about, and puzzled over it, and answered presently that he could feel it all right, but he couldn't see it.

"What *do* you see?" asked Wade. Davidson said he could see nothing but a lot of sand and broken-up shells. Wade gave him some other things to feel, telling him what they were, and watching him keenly.

"The ship is almost hull down," said Davidson, presently, *apropos* of nothing.

"Never mind the ship," said Wade. "Listen to me, Davidson. Do you know what hallucination means?"

"Rather," said Davidson.

"Well, everything you see is hallucinatory."

"Bishop Berkeley," said Davidson.

"Don't mistake me," said Wade. "You are alive, and in this room of Boyce's. But something has happened to your eyes. You cannot see; you can feel and hear, but not see. Do you follow me?"

"It seems to me that I see too much." Davidson rubbed his knuckles into his eyes. "Well?" he said.

"That's all. Don't let it perplex you. Bellows, here, and I will take you home in a cab."

"Wait a bit." Davidson thought. "Help me to sit down," said he, presently; "and now — I'm sorry to trouble you — but will 'you tell me all that over again?"

Wade repeated it very patiently. Davidson shut his eyes, and pressed his hands upon his forehead. "Yes," said he. "It's quite right. Now my eyes are shut I know you're right. That's you, Bellows, sitting by me on the couch. I'm in England again. And we're in the dark."

Then he opened his eyes. "And there," said he, "is the sun just rising, and the yards of the ship, and a tumbled sea, and a couple of birds flying. I never saw anything so real. And I'm sitting up to my neck in a bank of sand."

He bent forward and covered his face with his hands. Then he opened his eyes again. "Dark sea and sunrise! And yet I'm sitting on a sofa in old Boyce's room! — God help me!"

III

That was the beginning. For three weeks this strange affection of Davidson's eyes continued unabated. It was far worse than being blind. He was absolutely helpless, and had to be fed like a newly-hatched bird, and led about and undressed. If he attempted to move he fell over things or struck himself against walls or doors. After a day or so he got used to hearing our voices without seeing us, and willingly admitted he was at home, and that Wade was right in what he told him. My sister, to whom he was engaged, insisted on coming to see him, and would sit for hours every day while he talked about this beach of his. Holding her hand seemed to comfort him immensely. He explained that when we left the College and drove home, — he lived in Hampstead Village, — it appeared to him as if we drove right through a sandhill — it was perfectly black until he emerged again — and through rocks and trees and solid obstacles, and when he was taken to his own room it made him giddy and almost frantic with the fear of falling, because going upstairs seemed to lift him thirty or forty feet above the rocks of his imaginary island. He kept saying he should smash all the eggs. The end was that he had to be taken down into his father's consulting room and laid upon a couch that stood there.

He described the island as being a bleak kind of place on the whole, with very little vegetation, except some peaty stuff, and a lot of bare rock. There

were multitudes of penguins, and they made the rocks white and disagreeable to see. The sea was often rough, and once there was a thunderstorm,
and he lay and shouted at the silent flashes. Once or twice seals pulled up on
the beach, but only on the first two or three days. He said it was very funny
the way in which the penguins used to waddle right through him, and how
he seemed to lie among them without disturbing them.

I remember one odd thing, and that was when he wanted very badly to
smoke. We put a pipe in his hands — he almost poked his eye out with
it — and lit it. But he couldn't taste anything. I've since found it's the same
with me — I don't know if it's the usual case — that I cannot enjoy tobacco
at all unless I can see the smoke.

But the queerest part of his vision came when Wade sent him out in a
bath-chair to get fresh air. The Davidsons hired a chair, and got that deaf
and obstinate dependent of theirs, Widgery, to attend to it. Widgery's ideas
of healthy expeditions were peculiar. My sister, who had been to the Dog's
Home, met them in Camden Town, towards King's Cross. Widgery trotting
along complacently, and Davidson evidently most distressed, trying in his
feeble, blind way to attract Widgery's attention.

He positively wept when my sister spoke to him. "Oh, get me out of this
horrible darkness!" he said, feeling for her hand. "I must get out of it, or I
shall die." He was quite incapable of explaining what was the matter, but my
sister decided he must go home, and presently, as they went up the hill towards Hampstead, the horror seemed to drop from him. He said it was good
to see the stars again, though it was then about noon and a blazing day.

"It seemed," he told me afterwards, "as if I was being carried irresistibly
towards the water. I was not very much alarmed at first. Of course it was
night there — a lovely night."

"Of course?" I asked, for that struck me as odd.

"Of course," said he. "It's always night there when it is day here — Well,
we went right into the water, which was calm and shining under the moonlight — just a broad swell that seemed to grow broader and flatter as I came
down into it. The surface glistened just like a skin — it might have been
empty space underneath for all I could tell to the contrary. Very slowly, for I
rode slanting into it, the water crept up to my eyes. Then I went under, and
the skin seemed to break and heal again about my eyes. The moon gave a
jump up in the sky and grew green and dim, and fish, faintly glowing, came
darting round me — and things that seemed made of luminous glass, and I
passed through a tangle of seaweeds that shone with an oily lustre. And so I
drove down into the sea, and the stars went out one by one, and the moon
grew greener and darker, and the seaweed became a luminous purple-red.
It was all very faint and mysterious, and everything seemed to quiver. And

all the while I could hear the wheels of the bath-chair creaking, and the footsteps of people going by, and a man with a bell crying coals.

"I kept sinking down deeper and deeper into the water. It became inky black about me, not a ray from above came down into that darkness, and the phosphorescent things grew brighter and brighter. The snaky branches of the deeper weeds flickered like the flames of spirit lamps; but, after a time, there were no more weeds. The fishes came staring and gaping towards me, and into me and through me. I never imagined such fishes before. They had lines of fire along the sides of them as though they had been outlined with a luminous pencil. And there was a ghastly thing swimming backwards with a lot of twining arms. And then I saw, coming very slowly towards me through the gloom, a hazy mass of light that resolved itself as it drew nearer into multitudes of fishes, struggling and darting round something that drifted. I drove on straight towards it, and presently I saw in the midst of the tumult, and by the light of the fish, a bit of splintered spar looming over me, and a dark hull tilting over, and some glowing phosphorescent forms that were shaken and writhed as the fish bit at them. Then it was I began to try to attract Widgery's attention. A horror came upon me. Ugh! I should have driven right into those half-eaten — things. If your sister had not come! They had great holes in them, Bellows, and — Never mind. But it was ghastly!"

IV

For three weeks Davidson remained in this singular state, seeing what at the time we imagined was an altogether phantasmal world, and stone blind to the world around him. Then, one Tuesday, when I called, I met old Davidson in the passage. "He can see his thumb!" the old gentleman said, in a perfect transport. He was struggling into his overcoat. "He can see his thumb, Bellows!" he said, with the tears in his eyes. "The lad will be all right yet."

I rushed in to Davidson. He was holding up a little book before his face, and looking at it and laughing in a weak kind of way.

"It's amazing," said he. "There's a kind of patch come there." He pointed with his finger. "I'm on the rocks as usual, and the penguins are staggering and flapping about as usual, and there's been a whale showing every now and then, but it's got too dark now to make him out. But put something *there*, and I see it — I do see it. It's very dim and broken in places, but I see it all the same, like a faint spectre of itself. I found it out this morning while they were dressing me. It's like a hole in this infernal phantom world. Just put your hand by mine. No — not there. Ah! Yes! I see it. The base of your thumb and a bit of cuff! It looks like the ghost of a bit of your hand sticking out of the darkening sky. Just by it there's a group of stars like a cross coming out."

From that time Davidson began to mend. His account of the change, like his account of the vision, was oddly convincing. Over patches of his field of vision the phantom world grew fainter, grew transparent, as it were, and through these translucent gaps he began to see dimly the real world about him. The patches grew in size and number, ran together and spread until only here and there were blind spots left upon his eyes. He was able to get up and steer himself about, feed himself once more, read, smoke, and behave like an ordinary citizen again. At first it was very confusing to him to have these two pictures overlapping each other like the changing views of a lantern, but in a little while he began to distinguish the real from the illusory.

At first he was unfeignedly glad, and seemed only too anxious to complete his cure by taking exercise and tonics. But as that odd island of his began to fade away from him, he became queerly interested in it. He wanted particularly to go down into the deep sea again, and would spend half his time wandering about the low-lying parts of London, trying to find the water-logged wreck he had seen drifting. The glare of real daylight very soon impressed him so vividly as to blot out everything of his shadowy world, but of a nighttime, in a darkened room, he could still see the white-splashed rocks of the island, and the clumsy penguins staggering to and fro. But even these grew fainter and fainter, and, at last, soon after he married my sister, he saw them for the last time.

V

And now to tell of the queerest thing of all. About two years after his cure, I dined with the Davidsons, and after dinner a man named Atkins called in. He is a lieutenant in the Royal Navy, and a pleasant, talkative man. He was on friendly terms with my brother-in-law, and was soon on friendly terms with me. It came out that he was engaged to Davidson's cousin, and incidentally he took out a kind of pocket photograph case to show us a new rendering of his *fiancée*. "And, by-the-by," said he, "here's the old *Fulmar*."

Davidson looked at it casually. Then suddenly his face lit up. "Good heavens!" said he. "I could almost swear —"

"What?" said Atkins.

"That I had seen that ship before."

"Don't see how you can have. She hasn't been out of the South Seas for six years, and before then —"

"But," began Davidson, and then, "Yes — that's the ship I dreamt of. I'm sure that's the ship I dreamt of. She was standing off an island that swarmed with penguins, and she fired a gun."

"Good Lord!" said Atkins, who had never heard the particulars of the seizure. "How the deuce could you dream that?"

And then, bit by bit, it came out that on the very day Davidson was seized, H.M.S. *Fulmar* had actually been off a little rock to the south of Antipodes Island. A boat had landed overnight to get penguins' eggs, had been delayed, and a thunderstorm drifting up, the boat's crew had waited until the morning before rejoining the ship. Atkins had been one of them, and he corroborated, word for word, the descriptions Davidson had given of the island and the boat. There is not the slightest doubt in any of our minds that Davidson has really seen the place. In some unaccountable way, while he moved hither and thither in London, his sight moved hither and thither in a manner that corresponded, about this distant island. *How* is absolutely a mystery.

That completes the remarkable story of Davidson's eyes. It is perhaps the best authenticated case in existence of a real vision at a distance. Explanation there is none forthcoming, except what Professor Wade has thrown out. But his explanation invokes the Fourth Dimension, and a dissertation on theoretical kinds of space. To talk of there being "a kink in space" seems mere nonsense to me; it may be because I am no mathematician. When I said that nothing would alter the fact that the place is eight thousand miles away, he answered that two points might be a yard away on a sheet of paper and yet be brought together by bending the paper round. The reader may grasp his argument, but I certainly do not. His idea seems to be that Davidson, stooping between the poles of the big electro-magnet, had some extraordinary twist given to his retinal elements through the sudden change in the field of force due to the lightning.

He thinks, as a consequence of this, that it may be possible to live visually in one part of the world, while one lives bodily in another. He has even made some experiments in support of his views; but, so far, he has simply succeeded in blinding a few dogs. I believe that is the net result of his work, though I have not seen him for some weeks. Latterly, I have been so busy with my work in connection with the Saint Pancras installation that I have had little opportunity of calling to see him. But the whole of his theory seems fantastic to me. The facts concerning Davidson stand on an altogether different footing, and I can testify personally to the accuracy of every detail I have given.

UNDER THE KNIFE

Asleep under the influence of chloroform while undergoing a dangerous operation, the narrator has a vivid out-of-body dream. In his dream the operation is a failure and he dies. His spirit escapes from his body to travel outward through the solar system, through the Milky Way galaxy and finally leaves the universe altogether. Still soaring through the blackness, he sees the universe shrink to a glittering point of light reflected from a ring on the finger of a gigantic clenched hand!

This notion that our stars are atoms in a vaster universe, "and those again of another, and so on through an endless progression," later became a common science-fiction theme. In recent times Rudy Rucker has given it a bizarre topological twist. In one of his novels he imagines that the hierarchy of universes closes on itself. As you move outward through larger worlds, or downward through smaller ones, you eventually arrive back in the universe we know.

As Wells's dreamer travels through the solar system his time slows to a point where he sees the moon revolving rapidly around the earth. The story's description of the vast reaches of space-time, and the infinitesimal speck of matter on which we live, is Wells writing at his best. The story first appeared in *The New Review* (January 1896).

ᴧ

"WHAT if I die under it?" The thought recurred again and again as I walked home from Haddon's. It was a purely personal question. I was spared the deep anxieties of a married man, and I knew there were few of my intimate friends but would find my death troublesome chiefly on account of their duty of regret. I was surprised indeed and perhaps a little humiliated, as I turned the matter over, to think how few could possibly exceed the conventional requirement. Things came before me stripped of glamour, in a clear dry light, during that walk from Haddon's house over Primrose Hill. There were the friends of my youth; I perceived now that our affection was a tradition which we foregathered rather laboriously to maintain. There were the rivals and helpers of my later career: I suppose I had been cold-blooded or undemonstrative — one perhaps implies the other. It may be that even the capacity for friendship is a question of physique. There had been a time in my own life when I had grieved bitterly enough at the loss of a friend; but as I walked home that afternoon the emotional side of my imagination was dormant. I could not pity myself, nor feel sorry for my friends, nor conceive of them as grieving for me.

I was interested in this deadness of my emotional nature — no doubt a concomitant of my stagnating physiology; and my thoughts wandered off along the line it suggested. Once before, in my hot youth, I had suffered a sudden loss of blood and had been within an ace of death. I remembered now that my affections as well as my passions had drained out of me, leaving scarcely anything but a tranquil resignation, a dreg of self-pity. It had been weeks before the old ambitions, and tendernesses, and all the complex moral interplay of a man, had reasserted themselves. Now again I was bloodless; I had been feeding down for a week or more. I was not even hungry. It occurred to me that the real meaning of this numbness might be a gradual slipping away from the pleasure-pain guidance of the animal man. It has been proven, I take it, as thoroughly as anything can be proven in this world, that the higher emotions, the moral feelings, even the subtle tendernesses of love, are evolved from the elemental desires and fears of the simple animal: they are the harness in which man's mental freedom goes. And it may be that, as death overshadows us, as our possibility of acting diminishes, this complex growth of balanced impulse, propensity, and aversion whose interplay inspires our acts, goes with it. Leaving what?

I was suddenly brought back to reality by an imminent collision with a butcher-boy's tray. I found that I was crossing the bridge over the Regent's Park Canal which runs parallel with that in the Zoölogical Gardens. The boy in blue had been looking over his shoulder at a black barge advancing slowly, towed by a gaunt white horse. In the Gardens a nurse was leading three happy little children over the bridge. The trees were bright green; the spring hopefulness was still unstained by the dusts of summer; the sky in the water was bright and clear, but broken by long waves, by quivering bands of black, as the barge drove through. The breeze was stirring; but it did not stir me as the spring breeze used to do.

Was this dulness of feeling in itself an anticipation? It was curious that I could reason and follow out a network of suggestion as clearly as ever: so, at least, it seemed to me. It was calmness rather than dulness that was coming upon me. Was there any ground for the belief in the presentiment of death? Did a man near to death begin instinctively to withdraw himself from the meshes of matter and sense, even before the cold hand was laid upon his? I felt strangely isolated — isolated without regret — from the life and existence about me. The children playing in the sun and gathering strength and experience for the business of life, the park-keeper gossiping with a nursemaid, the nursing mother, the young couple intent upon each other as they passed me, the trees by the wayside spreading new pleading leaves to the sunlight, the stir in their branches — I had been part of it all, but I had nearly done with it now.

Some way down the Broad Walk I perceived that I was tired, and that my feet were heavy. It was hot that afternoon, and I turned aside and sat down on one of the green chairs that line the way. In a minute I had dozed into a dream, and the tide of my thoughts washed up a vision of the resurrection. I was still sitting in the chair, but I thought myself actually dead, withered, tattered, dried, one eye (I saw) pecked out by birds. "Awake!" cried a voice; and incontinently the dust of the path and the mould under the grass became insurgent. I had never before thought of Regent's Park as a cemetery, but now through the trees, stretching as far as eye could see, I beheld a flat plain of writhing graves and heeling tombstones. There seemed to be some trouble: the rising dead appeared to stifle as they struggled upward, they bled in their struggles, the red flesh was tattered away from the white bones. "Awake!" cried a voice; but I determined I would not rise to such horrors. "Awake!" They would not let me alone. "Wike up!" said an angry voice. A cockney angel! The man who sells the tickets was shaking me, demanding my penny.

I paid my penny, pocketed my ticket, yawned, stretched my legs, and, feeling now rather less torpid, got up and walked on towards Langham Place. I speedily lost myself again in a shifting maze of thoughts about death. Going across Marylebone Road into that crescent at the end of Langham Place, I had the narrowest escape from the shaft of a cab, and went on my way with a palpitating heart and a bruised shoulder. It struck me that it would have been curious if my meditations on my death on the morrow had led to my death that day.

But I will not weary you with more of my experiences that day and the next. I knew more and more certainly that I should die under the operation; at times I think I was inclined to pose to myself. At home I found everything prepared; my room cleared of needless objects and hung with white sheets; a nurse installed and already at loggerheads with my housekeeper. They wanted me to go to bed early, and after a little resistance I obeyed.

In the morning I was very indolent, and though I read my newspapers and the letters that came by the first post, I did not find them very interesting. There was a friendly note from Addison, my old school friend, calling my attention to two discrepancies and a printer's error in my new book, with one from Langridge venting some vexation over Minton. The rest were business communications. I had a cup of tea but nothing to eat. The glow of pain at my side seemed more massive. I knew it was pain, and yet, if you can understand, I did not find it very painful. I had been awake and hot and thirsty in the night, but in the morning bed felt comfortable. In the night-time I had lain thinking of things that were past; in the morning I dozed over the question of immortality. Haddon came, punctual to the minute, with a neat black bag; and Mowbray soon followed. Their arrival stirred me up a little. I began to take a more personal interest in the proceedings. Haddon moved the little octagonal table close to the bedside, and, with his broad black back to me, began taking things out of his bag. I heard the light click of steel upon steel. My imagination, I found, was not altogether stagnant. "Will you hurt me much?" I said in an off-hand tone.

"Not a bit," Haddon answered over his shoulder. "We shall chloroform you. Your heart's as sound as a bell." And as he spoke I had a whiff of the pungent sweetness of the anæsthetic.

They stretched me out, with a convenient exposure of my side, and, almost before I realised what was happening, the chloroform was being administered. It stings the nostrils, and there is a suffocating sensation, at first. I knew I should die — that this was the end of consciousness for me. And suddenly I felt that I was not prepared for death: I had a vague sense of a duty overlooked — I knew not what. What was it I had not done? I could think of nothing more to do, nothing desirable left in life; and yet I had the strangest disinclination for death. And the physical sensation was painfully oppressive. Of course the doctors did not know they were going to kill me. Possibly I struggled. Then I fell motionless, and a great silence, a monstrous silence, and an impenetrable blackness came upon me.

There must have been an interval of absolute unconsciousness, seconds or minutes. Then, with a chilly, unemotional clearness, I perceived that I was not yet dead. I was still in my body; but all the multitudinous sensations that come sweeping from it to make up the background of consciousness had gone, leaving me free of it all. No, not free of it all; for as yet something still held me to the poor stark flesh upon the bed — held me, yet not so closely that I did not feel myself external to it, independent of it, straining away from it. I do not think I saw, I do not think I heard; but I perceived all that was going on, and it was as if I both heard and saw. Haddon was bending over me, Mowbray behind me; the scalpel — it was a large scalpel — was cutting my flesh at the side under the flying ribs. It was interesting to see myself cut like cheese, without a pang, without even a qualm. The interest was much of a quality with that one might feel in a game of chess between strangers. Haddon's face was firm and his hand steady; but I was surprised to perceive (*how* I know not) that he was feeling the gravest doubt as to his own wisdom in the conduct of the operation.

Mowbray's thoughts, too, I could see. He was thinking that Haddon's manner showed too much of the specialist. New suggestions came up like bubbles through a stream of frothing meditation; and burst one after another in the little bright spot of his consciousness. He could not help noticing and admiring Haddon's swift dexterity, in spite of his envious quality and his disposition to detract. I saw my liver exposed. I was puzzled at my own condition. I did not feel that I was dead, but I was different in some way from my living self. The grey depression that had weighed on me for a year or more and coloured all my thoughts was gone. I perceived and thought without any emotional tint at all. I wondered if everyone perceived things in this way under chloroform, and forgot it again when he came out of it. It would be inconvenient to look into some heads, and not forget.

Although I did not think that I was dead, I still perceived quite clearly that I was soon to die. This brought me back to the consideration of Haddon's proceedings. I looked into his mind, and saw that he was afraid of cutting a branch of the portal vein. My attention was distracted from details by the curious changes going on in his mind. His consciousness was like the quivering little spot of light which is thrown by the mirror of a galvanometer. His thoughts ran under it like a stream, some through the focus bright and distinct, some shadowy in the half-light of the edge. Just now the little glow was steady; but the least movement on Mowbray's part, the slightest sound from outside, even a faint difference in the slow movement of the living flesh he was cutting, set the light-spot shivering and spinning. A new sense-impression came rushing up through the flow of thoughts, and lo! the light-spot jerked away towards it, swifter than a frightened fish. It was wonderful to think that upon that unstable, fitful thing depended all the complex motions of the man; that for the next five minutes, therefore, my life hung upon its movements. And he was growing more and more nervous in his work. It was as if a little picture of a cut vein grew brighter, and struggled to oust from his brain another picture of a cut falling short of the mark. He was afraid: his dread of cutting too little was battling with his dread of cutting too far.

Then, suddenly, like an escape of water from under a lock-gate, a great up-rush of horrible realisation set all his thoughts swirling, and simultaneously I perceived that the vein was cut. He started back with a hoarse exclamation, and I saw the brown-purple blood gather in a swift bead, and run trickling. He was horrified. He pitched the red stained scalpel on to the octagonal table; and instantly both doctors flung themselves upon me, making hasty and ill-conceived efforts to remedy the disaster. "Ice!" said Mowbray, gasping. But I knew that I was killed, though my body still clung to me.

I will not describe their belated endeavours to save me, though I perceived every detail. My perceptions were sharper and swifter than they had ever been in life; my thoughts rushed through my mind with incredible swiftness, but with perfect definition. I can only compare their crowded clarity to the effects of a reasonable dose of opium. In a moment it would all be over, and I should be free. I knew I was immortal, but what would happen I did not know. Should I drift off presently, like a puff of smoke from a gun, in some kind of half-material body, an attenuated version of my material self? Should I find myself suddenly among the innumerable hosts of the dead, and know the world about me for the phantasmagoria it had always seemed? Should I drift to some spiritualistic *séance*, and there make foolish, incomprehensible attempts to affect a purblind medium? It was a state of unemotional curiosity, of colourless expectation. And then I realised a growing stress upon me, a feeling as though some huge human magnet was drawing me upward out of my body. The stress grew and grew. I seemed an atom for which monstrous forces were fighting. For one brief, terrible moment sensation came back to me. That feeling of falling headlong which comes in nightmares, that feeling a thousand times intensified, that and a black horror swept across my thoughts in a torrent. Then the two doctors, the naked body with its cut side, the little room, swept away from under me and vanished as a speck of foam vanishes down an eddy.

I was in mid-air. Far below was the West End of London, receding rapidly, — for I seemed to be flying swiftly upward, — and, as it receded, passing westward, like a panorama. I could see, through the faint haze of smoke, the innumerable roofs chimney-set, the narrow roadways stippled with people and conveyances, the little specks of squares, and the church steeples like thorns sticking out of the fabric. But it spun away as the earth rotated on its axis, and in a few seconds (as it seemed) I was over the scattered clumps of town about Ealing, the little Thames a thread of blue to the south, and the Chiltern Hills and the North Downs coming up like the rim of a basin, far away and faint with haze. Up I rushed. And at first I had not the faintest conception what this headlong rush upward could mean.

Every moment the circle of scenery beneath me grew wider and wider, and the details of town and field, of hill and valley, got more and more hazy and pale and indistinct, a luminous grey was mingled more and more with the blue of the hills and the green of the open meadows; and a little patch of cloud, low and far to the west, shone ever more dazzlingly white. Above, as the veil of atmosphere between myself and outer space grew thinner, the sky, which had been a fair springtime blue at first, grew deeper and richer in colour, passing steadily through the intervening shades until presently it was as dark as the blue sky of midnight, and presently as black as the blackness of a frosty starlight, and at last as black as no blackness I had ever beheld. And first one star and then many, and at last an innumerable host broke out upon the sky: more stars than anyone has ever seen from the face of the earth. For the blueness of the sky is the light of the sun and stars sifted and spread abroad blindingly: there is diffused light even in the darkest skies of winter, and we do not see the stars by day only because of the dazzling irradiation of the sun. But now I saw things — I know not how; assuredly with no mortal eyes — and that defect of bedazzlement blinded me no longer. The sun was incredibly strange and wonderful. The body of it was a disc of blinding white light: not yellowish as it seems to those who live upon the earth, but livid white, all streaked with scarlet streaks and rimmed about with a fringe of writhing tongues of red fire. And, shooting halfway across the heavens from either side of it, and brighter than the Milky Way, were two pinions of silver-white, making it look more like those winged globes I have seen in Egyptian sculpture than anything else I can remember upon earth. These I knew for the solar corona, though I had never seen anything of it but a picture during the days of my earthly life.

When my attention came back to the earth again, I saw that it had fallen very far away from me. Field and town were long since indistinguishable, and all the varied hues of the country were merging into a uniform bright grey, broken only by the brilliant white of the clouds that lay scattered in flocculent masses over Ireland and the west of England. For now I could see the outlines of the north of France and Ireland, and all this island of Britain save where Scotland passed over the horizon to the north, or where the coast was blurred or obliterated by cloud. The sea was a dull grey, and darker than the land; and the whole panorama was rotating slowly towards the east.

All this had happened so swiftly that, until I was some thousand miles or so from the earth, I had no thought for myself. But now I perceived I had neither hands nor feet, neither parts nor organs, and that I felt neither alarm nor pain. All about me I perceived that the vacancy (for I had already left the air behind) was cold beyond the imagination of man; but it troubled me not. The sun's rays shot through the void, powerless to light or heat until they should strike on matter in their course. I saw things with a serene self-forgetfulness, even as if I were God. And down below there, rushing away from me, — countless miles in a second, — where a little dark spot on the grey marked the position of London, two doctors were struggling to restore life to the poor hacked and outworn shell I had abandoned. I felt then such release, such serenity as I can compare to no mortal delight I have ever known.

It was only after I had perceived all these things that the meaning of that headlong rush of the earth grew into comprehension. Yet it was so simple, so obvious, that I was amazed at my never anticipating the thing that was happening to me. I had suddenly been cut adrift from matter: all that was material of me was there upon earth, whirling away through space, held to the earth by gravitation, partaking of the earth's inertia, moving in its wreath of epicycles round the sun, and with the sun and the planets on their vast march through space. But the immaterial has no inertia, feels nothing of the pull of matter for matter: where it parts from its garments of flesh, there it remains (so far as space concerns it any longer) immovable in space. I was not leaving the earth: the earth was leaving *me*, and not only the earth, but the whole solar system was streaming past. And about me in space, invisible to me, scattered in the wake of the earth upon its journey, there must be an innumerable multitude of souls, stripped like myself of the material, stripped like myself of the passions of the individual and the generous emotions of the gregarious brute, naked intelligences, things of newborn wonder and thought, marvelling at the strange release that had suddenly come on them!

As I receded faster and faster from the strange white sun in the black heavens, and from the broad and shining earth upon which my being had begun, I seemed to grow, in some incredible manner, vast: vast as regards this world I had left, vast as regards the moments and periods of a human life. Very soon I saw the full circle of the earth, slightly gibbous, like the moon when she nears her full, but very large; and the silvery shape of America was now in the noonday blaze wherein (as it seemed) little England had been basking but minutes ago. At first the earth was large and shone in the heavens, filling a great part of them; but every moment she grew smaller and more distant. As she shrunk, the broad moon in its third quarter crept into view over the rim of her disc. I looked for the constellations. Only that part of Aries directly behind the sun, and the Lion, which the earth covered, were hidden. I recognised the tortuous, tattered band of the Milky Way, with Vega very bright between sun and earth; and Sirius and Orion shone splendid against the unfathomable blackness in the opposite quarter of the heavens. The Pole Star was overhead, and the Great Bear hung over the circle of the earth. And away beneath and beyond the shining corona of the sun were strange groupings of stars I had never seen in my life — notably, a dagger-shaped group that I knew for the Southern Cross. All these were no larger than when they had shone on earth; but the little stars that one scarcely sees shone now against the setting of black vacancy as brightly as the first-magnitudes had done, while the larger worlds were points of indescribable glory and colour. Aldebaran was a spot of blood-red fire, and Sirius condensed to one point the light of a world of sapphires. And they shone steadily: they did not scintillate, they were calmly glorious.

My impressions had an adamantine hardness and brightness: there was no blurring softness, no atmosphere, nothing but infinite darkness set with the myriads of these acute and brilliant points and specks of light. Presently, when I looked again, the little earth seemed no bigger than the sun, and it dwindled and turned as I looked until, in a second's space (as it seemed to me), it was halved; and so it went on swiftly dwindling. Far away in the opposite direction, a little pinkish pin's head of light, shining steadily, was the planet Mars. I swam motionless in vacancy, and, without a trace of terror or astonishment, watched the speck of cosmic dust we call the world fall away from me.

Presently it dawned upon me that my sense of duration had changed: that my mind was moving not faster but infinitely slower, that between each separate impression there was a period of many days. The moon spun once round the earth as I noted this; and I perceived clearly the motion of Mars in his orbit. Moreover, it appeared as if the time between thought and thought grew steadily greater, until at last, a thousand years was but a moment in my perception.

At first the constellations had shone motionless against the black background of infinite space; but presently it seemed as though the group of stars about Hercules and the Scorpion was contracting, while Orion and Aldebaran and their neighbours were scattering apart. Flashing suddenly out of the darkness there came a flying multitude of particles of rock, glittering like dust specks in a sunbeam, and encompassed in a faintly luminous haze. They swirled all about me, and vanished again in a twinkling far behind. And then I saw that a bright spot of light, that shone a little to one side of my path, was growing very rapidly larger, and perceived that it was the planet Saturn rushing towards me. Larger and larger it grew, swallowing up the heavens behind it, and hiding every moment a fresh multitude of stars. I perceived its flattened, whirling body, its disc-like belt, and seven of its little satellites. It grew and grew, till it towered enormous; and then I plunged amid a streaming multitude of clashing stones and dancing dust-particles and gas-eddies, and saw for a moment the mighty triple belt like three concentric arches of moonlight above me, its shadow black on the boiling tumult below. These things happened in one-tenth of the time it takes to tell of them. The planet went by like a flash of lightning; for a few seconds it blotted out the sun, and there and then became a mere black, dwindling, winged patch against the light. The earth, the mother mote of my being, I could no longer see.

So with a stately swiftness, in the profoundest silence, the solar system fell from me, as it had been a garment, until the sun was a mere star amid the multitude of stars, with its eddy of planet-specks, lost in the confused glittering of the remoter light. I was no longer a denizen of the solar system: I had come to the Outer Universe, I seemed to grasp and comprehend the whole world of matter. Ever more swiftly the stars closed in about the spot where Antares and Vega had vanished in a luminous haze, until that part of the sky had the semblance of a whirling mass of nebulæ, and ever before me yawned vaster gaps of vacant blackness and the stars shone fewer and fewer. It seemed as if I moved towards a point between Orion's belt and sword: and the void about that region opened vaster and vaster every second, an incredible gulf of nothingness, into which I was falling. Faster and ever faster the universe rushed by, a hurry of whirling motes at last, speeding silently into the void. Stars glowing brighter and brighter, with their circling planets catching the light in a ghostly fashion as I neared them, shone out and vanished again into inexistence; faint comets, clusters of meteorites, winking specks of matter, eddying light-points, whizzed past, some perhaps a hundred millions of miles or so from me at most, few nearer, travelling with unimaginable rapidity, shooting constellations, momentary darts of fire, through that black, enormous night. More than anything else it was like a dusty draught, sunbeam-lit. Broader, and wider, and deeper grew the starless space, the vacant Beyond, into which I was being drawn. At last a quarter of the heavens was black and blank, and the whole headlong rush of stellar universe closed in behind me like a veil of light that is gathered together. It drove away from me like a monstrous jack-o'-lantern driven by the wind. I had come out into the wilderness of space. Ever the vacant blackness grew broader, until the hosts of the stars seemed only like a swarm of fiery specks hurrying away from me, inconceivably remote, and the darkness, the nothingness and emptiness, was about me on every side. Soon the little universe of matter, the cage of points in which I had begun to be, was dwindling, now to a whirling disc of luminous glittering, and now to one minute disc of hazy light. In a little while it would shrink to a point, and at last would vanish altogether.

Suddenly feeling came back to me — feeling in the shape of overwhelming terror: such a dread of those dark vastitudes as no words can describe, a passionate resurgence of sympathy and social desire. Were there other souls, invisible to me as I to them, about me in the blackness? or was I indeed, even as I felt, alone? Had I passed out of being into something that was neither being nor not-being? The covering of the body, the covering of matter, had been torn from me, and the hallucinations of companionship and security. Everything was black and silent. I had ceased to be. I was nothing. There was nothing, save only that infinitesimal dot of light that dwindled in the gulf. I strained myself to hear and see, and for a while there was naught but infinite silence, intolerable darkness, horror, and despair.

Then I saw that about the spot of light into which the whole world of matter had shrunk there was a faint glow. And in a band on either side of that the darkness was not absolute. I watched it for ages, as it seemed to me, and through the long waiting the haze grew imperceptibly more distinct. And then about the band appeared an irregular cloud of the faintest, palest brown. I felt a passionate impatience; but the things grew brighter so slowly that they scarcely seemed to change. What was unfolding itself? What was this strange reddish dawn in the interminable night of space?

The cloud's shape was grotesque. It seemed to be looped along its lower side into four projecting masses, and, above, it ended in a straight line. What phantom was it? I felt assured I had seen that figure before; but I could not think what, nor where, nor when it was. Then the realisation rushed upon me. *It was a clenched Hand.* I was alone in space, alone with this huge, shadowy Hand, upon which the whole Universe of Matter lay like an unconsidered speck of dust. It seemed as though I watched it through vast periods of time. On the forefinger glittered a ring; and the universe from which I had come was but a spot of light upon the ring's curvature. And the thing that the hand gripped had the likeness of a black rod. Through a long eternity I watched this Hand, with the ring and the rod, marvelling and fearing and waiting helplessly on what might follow. It seemed as though nothing could follow: that I should watch for ever, seeing only the Hand and the thing it held, and understanding nothing of its import. Was the whole universe but a refracting speck upon some greater Being? Were our worlds but the atoms of another universe, and those again of another, and so on through an endless progression? And what was I? Was I indeed immaterial? A vague persuasion of a body gathering about me came into my suspense. The abysmal darkness about the Hand filled with impalpable suggestions, with uncertain, fluctuating shapes.

Came a sound, like the sound of a tolling bell; faint, as if infinitely far, muffled as though heard through thick swathings of darkness: a deep, vibrating resonance, with vast gulfs of silence between each stroke. And the Hand appeared to tighten on the rod. And I saw far above the Hand, towards the apex of the darkness, a circle of dim phosphorescence, a ghostly sphere whence these sounds came throbbing; and at the last stroke the Hand vanished, for the hour had come, and I heard a noise of many waters. But the black rod remained as a great band across the sky. And then a voice, which seemed to run to the uttermost parts of space, spoke, saying, "There will be no more pain."

At that an almost intolerable gladness and radiance rushed upon me, and I saw the circle shining white and bright, and the rod black and shining, and many things else distinct and clear. And the circle was the face of the clock, and the rod the rail of my bed. Haddon was standing at the foot, against the rail, with a small pair of scissors on his fingers; and the hands of my clock on the mantel over his shoulder were clasped together over the hour of twelve. Mowbray was washing something in a basin at the octagonal table, and at my side I felt a subdued feeling that could scarce be spoken of as pain.

The operation had not killed me. And I perceived, suddenly, that the dull melancholy of half a year was lifted from my mind.

THE QUEER STORY OF
BROWNLOW'S NEWSPAPER

H. G. Wells acquired a reputation as a prophet, and deservedly so because so many of his predictions came true. His greatest hit was his account of the discovery of how to unleash atomic energy and the use of what he called "atomic bombs" in a second world war triggered by Germany's invasion of France. All this in a novel, *The World Set Free*, published in 1914! There are many other remarkable hits in Wells's science fiction. For example, the steel sphere in his 1896 story "In the Abyss" allows a scientist to explore the bottom of the sea.

On the other hand, Wells had enormous misses. His greatest error was taking seriously the dubious reports of canals on Mars. They led Wells to introduce bizarre Martians in such novels as *The War of the Worlds* and in such stories as "The Crystal Egg." Of course hundreds of other science-fiction writers also wrote about Martians. Even in his serious nonfiction Wells made numerous bad guesses. Writing in 1901, in *Anticipations*, he did not think it probable that airplanes "will ever come into play as a serious modification of transport and communication."

In that same volume, in a chapter on twentieth-century warfare, Wells had this to say about submarines: "I must confess that my imagination, in spite even of spurring, refuses to see any sort of submarine doing anything but suffocate its crew and founder at sea." The chapter is filled with other blunders, although Wells correctly predicts that "the nation that will be the most powerful in warfare as in peace, will certainly be the ascendent or dominant nation before the year 2000."

In *The Way the World Is Going* (1928) Wells anticipated the "complete disappearance" of radio broadcasting, "confident that the unfortunate people, who must now subdue themselves to 'listening-in,' will soon find a better pastime for their leisure."

"The Queer Story of Brownlow's Newspaper" was a more mature Wells's attempt to describe England forty years in the future. It first appeared in, of all places, America's *Ladies' Home Journal* (April 1932). Almost forty years later, on November 10, 1971, London's *Evening Standard* reprinted the tale with comments on its hits and misses. Not surprisingly, no one named Evan O'Hara was found living in London. In the United States, on November 12, 1971, on the Long John Nebel radio talk show, science-fiction writers Frederik Pohl and Isaac Asimov discussed Wells's story.

Brownlow's newspaper is the usual Wells blend of good and bad prophecy. His hits are the widespread use of color in newspapers, the greater emphasis in the print media on science news and on psychological motivations, and the reduction of body clothing, though not to the extent of bare chests and breasts, or moving pockets to sleeves. Many people in Southwest Asia today do wear Western clothes. The Soviet empire has, happily, collapsed, as Wells expected, though this had not occurred by 1971.

Unfortunately, Wells's misses are far wider. Germany, France, England and the United States still flourish as nations. There is not the slightest sign of decreasing nationalism or the rise of a world government with police powerful enough to stop crime. The age of combustion has not been replaced by heat from the earth. Spelling has not been simplified. The stock market and financial pages have not become obsolete. The gorilla is not yet extinct. No thirteen-month calendar has been adopted.

Although some nations have curbed their birthrate, the world's rate is nowhere close to Wells's optimistic guesses. Newspapers are not printed on paper that is mostly aluminum. It is hard to comprehend how Wells failed to predict television, especially in view of the fact that Hugo Gernsback, who was enthusiastically reprinting Wells in *Amazing Stories*, actually ran a TV broadcast station in the twenties. The picture was tiny and people had to build their own sets, but the technology was rapidly advancing.

Brownlow's newspaper has nothing to say about atomic energy in spite of Wells's amazing anticipation of it in his *The World Set Free*. Space flight is also absent. Wells had earlier written a novel about a voyage to the moon but considered this one of his "impossible" fictions, never dreaming that such a trip would occur before the end of the century. Our astronauts walked on the moon in 1969. Ironically, Wells was a better prophet in his science fiction than in his more careful nonfiction efforts.

In 1933 Wells's most ambitious attempt to foresee the future was his thick book *The Shape of Things to Come*. It again is a mix of good and bad prophecy. The book makes no mention of the computer revolution, space flight, the discovery of DNA, the rise of television or the atomic age.

In Wells's introduction, Philip Raven, whose "dream book" is the basis for *The Shape of Things to Come*, describes his prophetic work as "rather like the newspaper of your friend Brownlow." Herbert George Wells could have ended his book the way he ended the story about Brownlow, by saying that he is as convinced of its accuracy as he is convinced that his name is Hubert G. Wells.

1

I CALL this a Queer Story because it is a story without an explanation. When I first heard it, in scraps, from Brownlow I found it queer and incredible. But — it refuses to remain incredible. After resisting and then questioning

and scrutinizing and falling back before the evidence, after rejecting al
his evidence as an elaborate mystification and refusing to hear any mor
about it, and then being drawn to reconsider it by an irresistible curiosit
and so going through it all again, I have been forced to the conclusion tha
Brownlow, so far as he can tell the truth, has been telling the truth. But i
remains queer truth, queer and exciting to the imagination. The more cred
ible his story becomes the queerer it is. It troubles my mind. I am fevered b
it, infected not with germs but with notes of interrogation and unsatisfie
curiosity.

Brownlow, is, I admit, a cheerful spirit. I have known him tell lies. Bu
I have never known him do anything so elaborate and sustained as this af
fair, if it is a mystification, would have to be. He is incapable of anything s
elaborate and sustained. He is too lazy and easy-going for anything of the
sort. And he would have laughed. At some stage he would have laughed anc
given the whole thing away. He has nothing to gain by keeping it up. Hi
honour is not in the case either way. And after all there is his bit of newspape
in evidence — and the scrap of an addressed wrapper. . . .

I realize it will damage this story for many readers that it opens witl
Brownlow in a state very definitely on the gayer side of sobriety. He was no
in a mood for cool and calculated observation, much less for accurate rec
ord. He was seeing things in an exhilarated manner. He was disposed to se
them and greet them cheerfully and let them slip by out of attention. The
limitations of time and space lay lightly upon him. It was after midnight. He
had been dining with friends.

I have inquired what friends — and satisfied myself upon one or two ob
vious possibilities of that dinner party. They were, he said to me, "jus
friends. They hadn't anything to do with it." I don't usually push past ar
assurance of this sort, but I made an exception in this case. I watchec
my man and took a chance of repeating the question. There was nothing
out of the ordinary about that dinner party, unless it was the fact that i
was an unusually good dinner party. The host was Redpath Baynes, the
solicitor, and the dinner was in his house in St. John's Wood. Gifford, o
the *Evening Telegraph*, whom I know slightly, was, I found, present, anc
from him I got all I wanted to know. There was much bright and discur
sive talk and Brownlow had been inspired to give an imitation of his aunt
Lady Clitherholme, reproving an inconsiderate plumber during some re
building operations at Clitherholme. This early memory had been receivec
with considerable merriment — he was always very good about his aunt
Lady Clitherholme — and Brownlow had departed obviously elated by thi
little social success and the general geniality of the occasion. Had the
talked, I asked, about the Future, or Einstein, or J.W. Dunne, or any such

high and serious topic at that party? They had not. Had they discussed the modern newspaper? No. There had been nobody whom one could call a practical joker at this party, and Brownlow had gone off alone in a taxi. That is what I was most desirous of knowing. He had been duly delivered by his taxi at the main entrance to Sussex Court.

Nothing untoward is to be recorded of his journey in the lift to the fifth floor of Sussex Court. The liftman on duty noted nothing exceptional. I asked if Brownlow said, "Good night." The liftman does not remember. "Usually he says Night O," reflected the liftman — manifestly doing his best and with nothing particular to recall. And there the fruits of my inquiries about the condition of Brownlow on this particular evening conclude. The rest of the story comes directly from him. My investigations arrive only at this: he was certainly not drunk. But he was lifted a little out of our normal harsh and grinding contact with the immediate realities of existence. Life was glowing softly and warmly in him, and the unexpected could happen brightly, easily, and acceptably.

He went down the long passage with its red carpet, its clear light, and its occasional oaken doors, each with its artistic brass number. I have been down that passage with him on several occasions. It was his custom to enliven that corridor by raising his hat gravely as he passed each entrance, saluting his unknown and invisible neighbours, addressing them softly but distinctly by playful if sometimes slightly indecorous names of his own devising, expressing good wishes or paying them little compliments.

He came at last to his own door, number 49, and let himself in without serious difficulty. He switched on his hall light. Scattered on the polished oak floor and invading his Chinese carpet were a number of letters and circulars, the evening's mail. His parlourmaid-housekeeper, who slept in a room in another part of the building, had been taking her evening out, or these letters would have been gathered up and put on the desk in his bureau. As it was, they lay on the floor. He closed his door behind him or it closed of its own accord; he took off his coat and wrap, placed his hat on the head of the Greek charioteer whose bust adorns his hall, and set himself to pick up his letters.

This also he succeeded in doing without misadventure. He was a little annoyed to miss the *Evening Standard*. It is his custom, he says, to subscribe for the afternoon edition of the *Star* to read at tea-time and also for the final edition of the *Evening Standard* to turn over the last thing at night, if only on account of Low's cartoon. He gathered up all these envelopes and packets and took them with him into his little sitting-room. There he turned on the electric heater, mixed himself a weak whisky-and-soda, went to his bedroom to put on soft slippers and replace his smoking jacket by a frogged jacket of llama wool, returned to his sitting-room, lit a cigarette, and sat down in his arm-chair by the reading lamp to examine his correspondence. He recalls all these details very exactly. They were routines he had repeated scores of times.

Brownlow's is not a preoccupied mind; it goes out to things. He is one of those buoyant extroverts who open and read all their letters and circulars whenever they can get hold of them. In the daytime his secretary intercepts and deals with most of them, but at night he escapes from her control and does what he pleases, that is to say, he opens everything.

He ripped up various envelopes. There was a formal acknowledgment of a business letter he had dictated the day before, there was a letter from his solicitor asking for some details about a settlement he was making, there was an offer from some unknown gentleman with an aristocratic name to lend him money on his note of hand alone, and there was a notice about a proposed new wing to his club. "Same old stuff," he sighed. "Same old stuff. What bores they all are!" He was always hoping, like every man who is proceeding across the plains of middle-age, that his correspondence would contain agreeable surprises — and it never did. Then, as he put it to me, *inter alia*, he picked up the remarkable newspaper.

2

It was different in appearance from an ordinary newspaper, but not so different as not to be recognizable as a newspaper, and he was surprised, he says, not to have observed it before. It was enclosed in a wrapper of pale green, but it was unstamped; apparently it had been delivered not by the postman, but by some other hand. (This wrapper still exists; I have seen it.) He had already torn it off before he noted that he was not the addressee.

For a moment or so he remained looking at this address, which struck him as just a little odd. It was printed in rather unusual type: "Evan O'Hara, Mr., Sussex Court 49."

"Wrong name," said Mr. Brownlow; "Right address. Rummy. Sussex Court 49. . . . 'Spose he's got *my Evening Standard*. . . . 'Change no robbery."

He put the torn wrapper with his unanswered letters and opened out the newspaper.

The title of the paper was printed in large slightly ornamental black-green letters that might have come from a kindred fount to that responsible for the address. But, as he read it, it was the *Evening Standard*! Or, at least, it was the "Even Standrd." "Silly," said Brownlow. "It's some damn Irish paper. Can't spell — anything — these Irish. . . ."

He had, I think, a passing idea, suggested perhaps by the green wrapper and the green ink, that it was a lottery stunt from Dublin.

Still, if there was anything to read he meant to read it. He surveyed the front page. Across this ran a streamer headline: "WILTON BORING REACHES SEVEN MILES: SUCCES ASSURED."

"No," said Brownlow. "It must be oil. . . . Illiterate lot these oil chaps — leave out the 's' in 'success.' "

He held the paper down on his knee for a moment, reinforced himself by a drink, took and lit a second cigarette, and then leant back in his chair to take a dispassionate view of any oil-share pushing that might be afoot.

But it wasn't an affair of oil. It was, it began to dawn upon him, something stranger than oil. He found himself surveying a real evening newspaper, which was dealing, so far as he could see at the first onset, with the affairs of another world.

He had for a moment a feeling as though he and his arm-chair and his little sitting-room were afloat in a vast space and then it all seemed to become firm and solid again.

This thing in his hands was plainly and indisputably a printed newspaper. It was a little odd in its letterpress, and it didn't feel or rustle like ordinary paper, but newspaper it was. It was printed in either three or four columns — for the life of him he cannot remember which — and there were column headlines under the page streamer. It had a sort of art-nouveau affair at the bottom of one column that might be an advertisement (it showed a woman in an impossibly big hat), and in the upper left-hand corner was an unmistakable weather chart of Western Europe, with *coloured* isobars, or isotherms, or whatever they are, and the inscription: "To-morrow's Weather."

And then he remarked the date. The date was November 10th, 1971!

"Steady on," said Brownlow. "Damitall! Steady on."

He held the paper sideways, and then straight again. The date remained November 10th, 1971.

He got up in a state of immense perplexity and put the paper down. For a moment he felt a little afraid of it. He rubbed his forehead. "Haven't been doing a Rip Van Winkle, by any chance, Brownlow, my boy?" he said. He picked up the paper again, walked out into his hall and looked at himself in the hall mirror. He was reassured to see no signs of advancing age, but the expression of mingled consternation and amazement upon his flushed face struck him suddenly as being undignified and unwarrantable. He laughed at himself, but not uncontrollably. Then he stared blankly at that familiar countenance. "I must be half-way *tordu*," he said, that being his habitual facetious translation of "screwed." On the console table was a little respectable-looking adjustable calendar bearing witness that the date was November 10th, 1931.

"D'you see?" he said, shaking the queer newspaper at it reproachfully. "I ought to have spotted you for a hoax ten minutes ago. 'Moosing trick, to say the least of it. I suppose they've made Low editor for a night, and he's had this idea. Eh?"

He felt he had been taken in, but that the joke was a good one. And, with quite unusual anticipations of entertainment, he returned to his arm-chair. A good idea it was, a paper forty years ahead. Good fun if it was well done. For a time nothing but the sounds of a newspaper being turned over and Brownlow's breathing can have broken the silence of the flat.

3

Regarded as an imaginative creation, he found the thing almost too well done. Every time he turned a page he expected the sheet to break out into laughter and give the whole thing away. But it did nothing of the kind. From being a mere quip, it became an immense and amusing, if perhaps a little over-elaborate, lark. And then, as a lark, it passed from stage to stage of incredibility until, as any thing but the thing it professed to be, it was incredible altogether. It must have cost far more than an ordinary number. All sorts of colours were used, and suddenly he came upon illustrations that went beyond amazement; they were in the colours of reality. Never in all his life had he seen such colour printing — and the buildings and scenery and costumes in the pictures were strange. Strange and yet credible. They were colour photographs of actuality forty years from now. He could not believe anything else of them. Doubt could not exist in their presence.

His mind had swung back, away from the stunt-number idea altogether. This paper in his hand would not simply be costly beyond dreaming to produce. At any price it could not be produced. All this present world could not produce such an object as this paper he held in his hand. He was quite capable of realizing that.

He sat turning the sheet over and — quite mechanically — drinking whisky. His sceptical faculties were largely in suspense; the barriers of criticism were down. His mind could now accept the idea that he was reading a newspaper of forty years ahead without any further protest.

It had been addressed to Mr. Evan O'Hara, and it had come to him. Well and good. This Evan O'Hara evidently knew how to get ahead of things. . . .

I doubt if at that time Brownlow found anything very wonderful in the situation.

Yet it was, it continues to be, a very wonderful situation. The wonder of

t mounts to my head as I write. Only gradually have I been able to build
up this picture of Brownlow turning over that miraculous sheet, so that I
can believe it myself. And you will understand how, as the thing flickered
between credibility and incredibility in my mind, I asked him, partly to jus-
ify or confute what he told me, and partly to satisfy a vast expanding and, at
last, devouring curiosity: "What was there in it? What did it have to say?" At
the same time, I found myself trying to catch him out in his story, and also
asking him for every particular he could give me.

What was there in it? In other words, What will the world be doing forty
years from now? That was the stupendous scale of the vision, of which
Brownlow was afforded a glimpse. The world forty years from now! I lie
awake at nights thinking of all that paper might have revealed to us. Much
t did reveal, but there is hardly a thing it reveals that does not change at
once into a constellation of riddles. When first he told me about the thing
  was — it is, I admit, an enormous pity — intensely sceptical. I asked him
questions in what people call a "nasty" manner. I was ready — as my manner made plain to him — to jump down his throat with "But that's prepos-
erous!" at the very first slip. And I had an engagement that carried me off at
the end of half an hour. But the thing had already got hold of my imagina-
ion, and I rang up Brownlow before tea-time, and was biting at this "queer
story" of his again. That afternoon he was sulking because of my morning's
disbelief, and he told me very little. "I was drunk and dreaming, I suppose,"
he said. "I'm beginning to doubt it all myself." In the night it occurred to
me for the first time that, if he was not allowed to tell and put on record
what he had seen, he might become both confused and sceptical about it
himself. Fancies might mix up with it. He might hedge and alter to get it
more credible. Next day, therefore, I lunched and spent the afternoon with
him, and arranged to go down into Surrey for the week-end. I managed to
dispel his huffiness with me. My growing keenness restored his. There we
set ourselves in earnest, first of all to recover everything he could remember about his newspaper and then to form some coherent idea of the world
about which it was telling.

It is perhaps a little banal to say we were not trained men for the job.
For who could be considered trained for such a job as we were attempt-
ing? What facts was he to pick out as important and how were they to be
arranged? We wanted to know everything we could about 1971; and the
little facts and the big facts crowded on one another and offended against
each other.

The streamer headline across the page about that seven-mile Wilton boring, is, to my mind, one of the most significant items in the story. About
that we are fairly clear. It referred, says Brownlow, to a series of attempts
to tap the supply of heat beneath the surface of the earth. I asked various

questions. "It was *explained*, y'know," said Brownlow, and smiled and held out a hand with twiddling fingers. "It was explained all right. Old system, they said, was to go down from a few hundred feet to a mile or so and bring up coal and burn it. Go down a bit deeper, and there's no need to bring up and burn anything. Just get heat itself straightaway. Comes up of its own accord — under its own steam. See? Simple.

"They were making a big fuss about it," he added. "It wasn't only the streamer headline; there was a leading article in big type. What was it headed? Ah! The Age of Combustion Has Ended!"

Now that is plainly a very big event for mankind, caught in mid-happening, November 10th, 1971. And the way in which Brownlow describes it as being handled, shows clearly a world much more preoccupied by economic essentials than the world of to-day, and dealing with them on a larger scale and in a bolder spirit.

That excitement about tapping the central reservoirs of heat, Brownlow was very definite, was not the only symptom of an increase in practical economic interest and intelligence. There was much more space given to scientific work and to inventions than is given in any contemporary paper. There were diagrams and mathematical symbols, he says, but he did not look into them very closely because he could not get the hang of them. "*Frightfully* highbrow, some of it," he said.

A more intelligent world for our grandchildren evidently, and also, as the pictures testified, a healthier and happier world.

"The fashions kept you looking," said Brownlow, going off at a tangent, "all coloured up as they were."

"Were they elaborate?" I asked.

"Anything *but*," he said.

His description of these costumes is vague. The people depicted in the social illustrations and in the advertisements seemed to have reduced body clothing — I mean things like vests, pants, socks and so forth — to a minimum. Breast and chest went bare. There seem to have been tremendously exaggerated wristlets, mostly on the left arm and going as far up as the elbow, provided with gadgets which served the purpose of pockets. Most of these armlets seem to have been very decorative, almost like little shields. And then, usually, there was an immense hat, often rolled up and carried in the hand, and long cloaks of the loveliest colours and evidently also of the most beautiful soft material, which either trailed from a sort of gorget or were gathered up and wrapped about the naked body, or were belted up and thrown over the shoulders.

There were a number of pictures of crowds from various parts of the world. "The people looked fine," said Brownlow. "Prosperous, you know, and upstanding. Some of the women — just lovely."

My mind went off to India. What was happening in India?

Brownlow could not remember anything very much about India. "Ankor," said Brownlow. "That's not India, is it?" There had been some sort of Carnival going on amidst "perfectly lovely" buildings in the sunshine of Ankor.

The people there were brownish people but they were dressed very much like the people in other parts of the world.

I found the politician stirring in me. Was there really nothing about India? Was he sure of that? There was certainly nothing that had left any impression in Brownlow's mind. And Soviet Russia? "Not as Soviet Russia," said Brownlow. All that trouble had ceased to be a matter of daily interest. "And how was France getting on with Germany?" Brownlow could not recall a mention of either of these two great powers. Nor of the British Empire as such, nor of the U.S.A. There was no mention of any interchanges, communications, ambassadors, conferences, competitions, comparisons, stresses, in which these governments figured, so far as he could remember. He racked his brains. I thought perhaps all that had been going on so entirely like it goes on to-day — and has been going on for the last hundred years — that he had run his eyes over the passages in question and that they had left no distinctive impression on his mind. But he is positive that it was not like that. "All that stuff was washed out," he said. He is unshaken in his assertion that there were no elections in progress, no notice of Parliament or politicians, no mention of Geneva or anything about armaments or war. All those main interests of a contemporary journal seem to have been among the "washed out" stuff. It isn't that Brownlow didn't notice them very much; he is positive they were not there.

Now to me this is a very wonderful thing indeed. It means, I take it, that in only forty years from now the great game of sovereign states will be over. It looks also as if the parliamentary game will be over, and as if some quite new method of handling human affairs will have been adopted. Not a word of patriotism or nationalism; not a word of party, not an allusion. But in only forty years! While half the human beings already alive in the world will still be living! You cannot believe it for a moment. Nor could I, if it wasn't for two little torn scraps of paper. These, as I will make clear, leave me in a state of — how can I put it? — incredulous belief.

4

After all, in 1831 very few people thought of railway or steamship travel, and in 1871 you could already go round the world in eighty days by steam, and send a telegram in a few minutes to nearly every part of the earth. Who would have thought of that in 1831? Revolutions in human life, when they begin to come, can come very fast. Our ideas and methods change faster than we know.

But just forty years!

It was not only that there was this absence of national politics from that evening paper, but there was something else still more fundamental. Business, we both think, finance that is, was not in evidence, at least upon anything like contemporary lines. We are not quite sure of that, but that is our impression. There was no list of Stock Exchange prices, for example, no City page, and nothing in its place. I have suggested already that Brownlow just turned that page over, and that it was sufficiently like what it is to-day that he passed and forgot it. I have put that suggestion to him. But he is quite sure that that was not the case. Like most of us nowadays, he is watching a number of his investments rather nervously, and he is convinced he looked for the City article.

November 10th, 1971, may have been Monday — there seems to have been some readjustment of the months and the days of the week; that is a detail into which I will not enter now — but that will not account for the absence of any City news at all. That also, it seems, will be washed out forty years from now.

Is there some tremendous revolutionary smash-up ahead, then? Which will put an end to investment and speculation? Is the world going Bolshevik? In the paper, anyhow, there was no sign of, or reference to, anything of that kind. Yet against this idea of some stupendous economic revolution we have the fact that here forty years ahead is a familiar London evening paper still tumbling into a private individual's letter-box in the most uninterrupted manner. Not much suggestion of a social smash-up there. Much stronger is the effect of immense changes which have come about bit by bit, day by day, and hour by hour, without any sort of revolutionary jolt, as morning or springtime comes to the world.

These futile speculations are irresistible. The reader must forgive me them. Let me return to our story.

There had been a picture of a landslide near Ventimiglia and one of some new chemical works at Salzburg, and there had been a picture of fighting going on near Irkutsk. (Of that picture, as I will tell presently, a fading scrap survives.) "Now that was called —" Brownlow made an effort, and snapped his fingers triumphantly. "— 'Round-up of Brigands by Federal Police.'"

"*What* Federal Police?" I asked.

"There you have me," said Brownlow. "The fellows on both sides looked mostly Chinese, but there were one or two taller fellows, who might have been Americans or British or Scandinavians.

"What filled a lot of the paper," said Brownlow, suddenly, "was gorillas. There was no end of a fuss about gorillas. Not so much as about that boring, but still a lot of fuss. Photographs. A map. A special article and some paragraphs."

The paper, had, in fact, announced the death of the last gorilla. Considerable resentment was displayed at the tragedy that had happened in the African gorilla reserve. The gorilla population of the world had been dwindling for many years. In 1931 it had been estimated at nine hundred. When the Federal Board took over it had shrunken to three hundred.

"*What* Federal Board?" I asked.

Brownlow knew no more than I did. When he read the phrase, it had seemed all right somehow. Apparently this Board had had too much to do all at once, and insufficient resources. I had the impression at first that it must be some sort of conservation board, improvised under panic conditions, to save the rare creatures of the world threatened with extinction. The gorillas had not been sufficiently observed and guarded, and they had been swept out of existence suddenly by a new and malignant form of influenza. The thing had happened practically before it was remarked. The paper was clamouring for inquiry and drastic changes of reorganization.

This Federal Board, whatever it might be, seemed to be something of very considerable importance in the year 1971. Its name turned up again in an article of afforestation. This interested Brownlow considerably because he has large holdings in lumber companies. This Federal Board was apparently not only responsible for the maladies of wild gorillas but also for the plantation of trees in — just note these names! — Canada, New York State, Siberia, Algiers, and the East Coast of England, and it was arraigned for various negligences in combating insect pests and various fungoid plant diseases. It jumped all our contemporary boundaries in the most astounding way. Its range was world-wide. "In spite of the recent additional restrictions put upon the use of big timber in building and furnishing, there is a plain possibility of a shortage of shelter timber and of rainfall in nearly all the threatened regions for 1985 onwards. Admittedly the Federal Board has come late to its task, from the beginning its work has been urgency work; but in view of the lucid report prepared by the James Commission, there is little or no excuse for the inaggressiveness and overconfidence it has displayed."

I am able to quote this particular article because as a matter of fact it lies before me as I write. It is indeed, as I will explain, all that remains of this remarkable newspaper. The rest has been destroyed and all we can ever know of it now is through Brownlow's sound but not absolutely trustworthy memory.

5

My mind, as the days pass, hangs on to that Federal Board. Does that phrase mean, as just possibly it may mean, a world federation, a scientific control of all human life only forty years from now? I find that idea — staggering. I have always believed that the world was destined to unify — "Parliament of Mankind and Confederation of the World," as Tennyson put it — but I have always supposed that the process would take centuries. But then my time sense is poor. My disposition has always been to under-estimate the pace of change. I wrote in 1900 that there would be aeroplanes "in fifty years' time." And the confounded things were buzzing about everywhere and carrying passengers before 1920.

Let me tell very briefly of the rest of that evening paper. There seemed to be a lot of sport and fashion; much about something called "Specta-cle" — with pictures — a lot of illustrated criticism of decorative art and particularly of architecture. The architecture in the pictures he saw was "towering — kind of magnificent. Great blocks of building. New York, but more so and all run together" . . . Unfortunately he cannot sketch. There were sections devoted to something he couldn't understand, but which he thinks was some sort of "radio programme stuff."

All that suggests a sort of advanced human life very much like the life we lead to-day, possibly rather brighter and better.

But here is something — different.

"The birth-rate," said Brownlow, searching his mind, "was seven in the thousand."

I exclaimed. The lowest birth-rates in Europe now are sixteen or more per thousand. The Russian birth-rate is forty per thousand, and falling slowly.

"It was seven," said Brownlow. "Exactly seven. I noticed it. In a para-graph."

But what birth-rate, I asked. The British? The European?

"It said the birth-rate," said Brownlow. "Just that."

That I think is the most tantalizing item in all this strange glimpse of the world of our grandchildren. A birth-rate of seven in the thousand does not mean a fixed world population; it means a population that is being reduced at a very rapid rate — unless the death-rate has gone still lower. Quite pos-sibly people will not be dying so much then, but living very much longer. On that Brownlow could throw no light. The people in the pictures did not look to him an "old lot." There were plenty of children and young or young-looking people about.

"But Brownlow," I said, "wasn't there any crime?"

"Rather," said Brownlow. "They had a big poisoning case on, but it was jolly hard to follow. You know how it is with these crimes. Unless you've read about it from the beginning, it's hard to get the hang of the situation. No newspaper has found out that for every crime it ought to give a summary up-to-date every day — and forty years ahead, they hadn't. Or they aren't going to. Whichever way you like to put it.

"There were several crimes and what newspaper men call stories," he resumed; "personal stories. What struck me about it was that they seemed to be more sympathetic than our reporters, more concerned with the motives and less with just finding someone out. What you might call psychological — so to speak."

"Was there anything much about books?" I asked him.

"I don't remember anything about books," he said. . . .

And that is all. Except for a few trifling details such as a possible thirteenth month inserted in the year, that is all. It is intolerably tantalizing. That is the substance of Brownlow's account of his newspaper. He read it — as one might read any newspaper. He was just in that state of alcoholic comfort when nothing is incredible and so nothing is really wonderful. He knew he was reading an evening newspaper of forty years ahead and he sat in front of his fire, and smoked and sipped his drink and was no more perturbed than he would have been if he had been reading an imaginative book about the future.

Suddenly his little brass clock pinged Two.

He got up and yawned. He put that astounding, that miraculous newspaper down as he was wont to put any old newspaper down; he carried off his correspondence to the desk in his bureau, and with the swift laziness of a very tired man he dropped his clothes about his room anyhow and went to bed.

But somewhen in the night he woke up feeling thirsty and grey-minded. He lay awake and it came to him that something very strange had occurred to him. His mind went back to the idea that he had been taken in by a very ingenious fabrication. He got up for a drink of Vichy water and a liver tabloid, he put his head in cold water and found himself sitting on his bed towelling his hair and doubting whether he had really seen those photographs in the very colours of reality itself, or whether he had imagined them. Also running through his mind was the thought that the approach of a world timber famine for 1985 was something likely to affect his investments and particularly a trust he was setting up on behalf of an infant in whom he was interested. It might be wise, he thought, to put more into timber.

He went back down the corridor to his sitting-room. He sat there in his dressing-gown, turning over the marvellous sheets. There it was in his hands complete in every page, not a corner torn. Some sort of auto-hypnosis, he thought, might be at work, but certainly the pictures seemed as real as looking out of a window. After he had stared at them some time he went back to the timber paragraph. He felt he must keep that. I don't know if you will understand how his mind worked — for my own part I can see at once how perfectly irrational and entirely natural it was — but he took this marvellous paper, creased the page in question, tore off this particular article and left the rest. He returned very drowsily to his bedroom, put the scrap of paper on his dressing-table, got into bed and dropped off to sleep at once.

6

When he awoke it was nine o'clock; his morning tea was untasted by his bedside and the room was full of sunshine. His parlourmaid-housekeeper had just re-entered the room.

"You were sleeping so peacefully," she said; "I couldn't bear to wake you. Shall I get you a fresh cup of tea?"

Brownlow did not answer. He was trying to think of something strange that had happened.

She repeated her question.

"No. I'll come and have breakfast in my dressing-gown before my bath," he said, and she went out of the room.

Then he saw the scrap of paper.

In a moment he was running down the corridor to the sitting-room. "I left a newspaper," he said. "I left a newspaper."

She came in response to the commotion he made.

"A newspaper?" she said. "It's been gone this two hours, down the chute, with the dust and things."

Brownlow had a moment of extreme consternation.

He invoked his God. "I wanted it *kept!*" he shouted. "I wanted it *kept.*"

"But how was *I* to know you wanted it kept?"

"But didn't you notice it was a very extraordinary-looking newspaper?"

"I've got none too much time to dust out this flat to be looking at newspapers," she said. "I thought I saw some coloured photographs of bathing ladies and chorus girls in it, but that's no concern of mine. It didn't seem a proper newspaper to me. How was I to know you'd be wanting to look at them again this morning?"

"I must get that newspaper back," said Brownlow. "It's — it's vitally important . . . If all Sussex Court has to be held up I want that newspaper back."

"I've never known a thing come up that chute again," said his house-keeper, "that's once gone down it. But I'll telephone down, sir, and see what can be done. Most of that stuff goes right into the hot-water furnace, they say. . . ."

It does. The newspaper had gone.

Brownlow came near raving. By a vast effort of self-control he sat down and consumed his cooling breakfast. He kept on saying "Oh, my God!" as he did so. In the midst of it he got up to recover the scrap of paper from his bedroom, and then found the wrapper addressed to Evan O'Hara among the overnight letters on his bureau. That seemed an almost maddening confirmation. The thing *had* happened.

Presently after he had breakfasted, he rang me up to aid his baffled mind.

I found him at his bureau with the two bits of paper before him. He did not speak. He made a solemn gesture.

"What is it?" I asked, standing before him.

"Tell me," he said. "Tell me. What are these objects? It's serious. Either —" He left the sentence unfinished.

I picked up the torn wrapper first and felt its texture. "Evan O'Hara, Mr.," I read.

"Yes. Sussex Court, 49. Eh?"

"Right," I agreed and stared at him.

"*That's* not hallucination, eh?"

I shook my head.

"And now this?" His hand trembled as he held out the cutting. I took it.

"Odd," I said. I stared at the black-green ink, the unfamiliar type, the little novelties in spelling. Then I turned the thing over. On the back was a piece of one of the illustrations; it was, I suppose, about a quarter of the photograph of that "Round-up of Brigands by Federal Police" I have already mentioned.

When I saw it that morning it had not even begun to fade. It represented a mass of broken masonry in a sandy waste with bare-looking mountains in the distance. The cold, clear atmosphere, the glare of a cloudless after-noon were rendered perfectly. In the foreground were four masked men in a brown service uniform intent on working some little machine on wheels with a tube and a nozzle projecting a jet that went out to the left, where the fragment was torn off. I cannot imagine what the jet was doing. Brownlow says he thinks they were gassing some men in a hut. Never have I seen such realistic colour printing.

"What on earth is this?" I asked.

"It's *that*," said Brownlow. "I'm not mad, am I? It's really *that*."

"But what the devil is it?"

"It's a piece of newspaper for November 10th, 1971."

"You had better explain," I said, and sat down, with the scrap of paper in my hand, to hear his story. And, with as much elimination of questions and digressions and repetitions as possible, that is the story I have written here.

I said at the beginning that it was a queer story and queer to my mind it remains, fantastically queer. I return to it at intervals, and it refuses to settle down in my mind as anything but an incongruity with all my experience and beliefs. If it were not for the two little bits of paper, one might dispose of it quite easily. One might say that Brownlow had had a vision, a dream of unparalleled vividness and consistency. Or that he had been hoaxed and his head turned by some elaborate mystification. Or, again, one might suppose he had really seen into the future with a sort of exaggeration of those previsions cited by Mr. J. W. Dunne in his remarkable "Experiment with Time." But nothing Mr. Dunne has to advance can account for an actual evening paper being slapped through a letter-slit forty years in advance of its date.

The wrapper has not altered in the least since I first saw it. But the scrap of paper with the article about afforestation is dissolving into a fine powder and the fragment of picture at the back of it is fading out; most of the colour has gone and the outlines have lost their sharpness. Some of the powder I have taken to my friend Ryder at the Royal College, whose work in microchemistry is so well known. He says the stuff is not paper at all, properly speaking. It is mostly aluminium fortified by admixture with some artificial resinous substance.

7

Though I offer no explanation whatever of this affair I think I will venture on one little prophesy. I have an obstinate persuasion that on November 10th, 1971, the name of the tenant of 49, Sussex Court, will be Mr. Evan O'Hara. (There is no tenant of that name now in Sussex Court and I find no evidence in the Telephone Directory, or the London Directory, that such a person exists anywhere in London.) And on that particular evening forty years ahead, he will not get his usual copy of the *Even Standrd:* instead he will get a copy of the *Evening Standard* of 1931. I have an incurable fancy that this will be so.

There I may be right or wrong, but that Brownlow really got and for two remarkable hours, read, a real newspaper forty years ahead of time I am as convinced as I am convinced that my own name is Hubert G. Wells. Can I say anything stronger than that?